Just the Way You Are

Dunlin shores
Book one

Ann Roth

Cover by Elaina Lee, For the Muse Design:
www.forthemusedesign.com

Formatting by BB eBooks:
bbebooksthailand.com

**Find out about new releases! Sign up for my newsletter
http://bit.ly/2WxhNQT**

How can she resist?

After a painful breakup and the loss of her job, Cinnamon Smith feels battered and bruised. The only place to go is her best friend Fran's bed-and-breakfast in the small coastal town of Dunlin Shores, Oregon. The first person she meets on her arrival is Nick Mahoney, Fran's handyman. Cinnamon's attraction to Nick is immediate, and the feeling is definitely mutual.

But Cinnamon has spent years working toward a certain kind of life, a life she can't have with Nick. Spending time in Dunlin Shores and with him is beginning to change all that. Then she gets a job offer that will put her career goals back on track... Which means choosing between the life she's always wanted and the love that's right in front of her.

Chapter One

THE BEAM OF Cinnamon Smith's headlights cut through the darkness and the misty rain, illuminating a painted sign. *Oceanside Bed and Breakfast*, it proclaimed in cheerfully scripted letters.

After five years of listening to Fran rave about the bed and breakfast she'd inherited, Cinnamon was finally here. Sighing with relief—she'd been on the road a good four hours since flying into Portland from L.A.—she drove her rented compact up the gravel driveway.

For the past four months she'd lived in a state of perpetual tension and misery. The last two weeks had been especially bad, and she could hardly wait to relax and unwind. As she neared the building floodlights blinked on, bathing the shingled house in bright light. She braked to a stop in the large guest parking area beside the garage. Aside from a battered red pickup, hers was the only vehicle.

Small wonder. Late January wasn't exactly tourist

season on the Oregon coast. The truck, she assumed, belonged to the man who Fran told her did odd jobs around the place. Why was he here after dark?

As the inn's only guest, Cinnamon looked forward to cozy evenings with her best friend and much-needed heart-to-hearts. Fran was solid and down-to-earth, and Cinnamon needed her calming influence. All two weeks of it. Actually, thirteen days, but close enough.

Cold mist bathed her face as she exited the car and stretched for the first time in hours. Slinging the strap of her purse over her shoulder, she squinted past the bright circle of light for a glimpse of the ocean. It was too dark to see anything, but she smelled the sea's salty tang and heard the gentle slap of the waves. She could hardly wait to walk the beach.

She was counting on the change of scenery to help her put the past behind her. Maybe then she'd be able to move on. She also needed to find a new job. Since resigning as a consultant at Sabin and Howe three days ago, which beat getting fired, she'd been at loose ends, aimless and scared.

Two months' salary in savings wouldn't last long. As she opened the rear door of the compact, the familiar panicky feeling—racing heart and nausea—threatened to overwhelm her.

She made herself take a deep breath. Much better. There were plenty of companies in the world as good or better than Sabin and Howe. Hadn't she recently sent out emails to friends and colleagues in big consulting firms all over the country? Surely one of them knew of a job opening.

The thought filled her with hope, so much so that her stomach growled from hunger, a welcome change from weeks of no appetite. She retrieved her laptop and toiletries case, then swung those straps onto the other shoulder. Only the jumbo-size suitcase remained. She opened the trunk, grabbed the handle and tugged. Filled with a parka, clothing, shoes, and a pile of paperbacks she meant to read, it weighed a good forty pounds. No problem, she was strong. Still, she grunted with effort.

"I'll get that."

The large male at her side startled her. She hadn't heard him approach.

Gently nudging her over, he reached for the suitcase, his big, warm hand closing over her cold fist. Taken aback and not about to relinquish her bag, she tightened her grip and shot him the intimidating look that'd helped hone her the reputation as shrewd and not easily pushed around.

"Who are you?" In the chill dampness, her breath

ANN ROTH

clouded.

He released his hand and stepped aside. "My name's Nick Mahoney. I work for Fran. I was on my way to the truck to head home, and figured you could use a hand."

Thanks to the floodlights she noted his striking blue eyes. His straight nose and generous mouth also ranked at the top of the handsome scale.

"Fran talks about you all the time. Sorry I was rude."

His gaze flickered over her, calf-length leather coat and all. Though still half bent over the suitcase, she sucked in her stomach.

The corner of his mouth lifted, charming her.

"Apology accepted."

"I… I'm Cinnamon Smith," she managed, suddenly wishing she'd combed her hair and freshened her makeup. She thought about shaking his hand, but decided against it and kept her fingers wrapped firmly around the handle of her suitcase.

"I know who you are. Fran's been talking about your visit since last Friday."

"Really. What did she tell you?" Cinnamon trusted her friend not to reveal the details of her messy life, but she was curious.

"That you two met in college and shared an apartment after, and that you haven't seen each other since

4

she moved here and you became a hotshot executive. She's real excited about this visit." He flirted with a grin as if he also looked forward to her being here.

Holy moly, the man had a dimple in his cheek. Fran had never mentioned his looks. Was she blind?

"Are you going to let go of that bag, or would you rather carry it yourself?"

Her face felt hot and she knew she was blushing. "You go ahead." She released the handle and straightened. "Thanks."

"My pleasure," he drawled.

Fran hadn't mentioned he was a flirt either. Cinnamon was less than skilled at the art, and anyway, she was through with men. For a while, at least. When she did decide to date again, she intended to find an upwardly mobile, career-focused, marriage-minded male. This time, single. Not a handyman, no matter how attractive he was.

He extracted the heavy suitcase as if it were as light as a sea breeze, and nodded toward the bed and breakfast. "The front door's on the ocean side of the house."

He strode forward. Cinnamon trailed him around the building. Seemingly heedless of the winter chill, he wore no coat over his long-sleeved T-shirt and jeans. He was a big man with big limbs. Not heavy, but muscled and solid.

"You must be freezing," she said. "Where's your coat?"

"Left it in the truck."

Despite being in excellent physical condition—she jogged three days a week—Cinnamon was slightly breathless, and not from the climb. She snickered at that.

She was here to pull herself together, and look for work with a new employer in a big city. She didn't need or want the distraction of any man.

Her gaze dropped to his rear end and powerful legs. My, oh, my…

Stop that. Any woman with eyes would lust after the gorgeous male leading the way.

Although it felt like ages since she'd noticed. She hadn't had sex, let along looked at a man, since Dwight had dropped her cold four months earlier. This after repeatedly assuring her that his divorce was imminent and he wanted to marry her. Instead, he'd stunned her with the news that he and his wife had reconciled.

The lying rat. His change of heart had pretty much ruined her reputation at Sabin and Howe. Determined to weather the scandal, she'd powered on. But her client load shrank and she understood that if she didn't resign she'd be terminated.

And there she was, all tense again. Another deep breath helped. That was in the past now. Starting this very minute, she would forge ahead toward a new and better life.

With her chin raised, she followed Nick up the steps.

CINNAMON LIKED THE tiny white lights along the hand railing leading to the Oceanside's front door. "This is charming."

"Wait till morning when you see the ocean view from the deck off the dining room," Nick replied with a nod toward the darkness beyond.

The front door was painted a warm purple. The whimsical pelican-shaped metal knocker and the decorative heart wreath woven of sticks were so like Fran that Cinnamon smiled.

Nick wiped his feet on the thick mat, also purple, and opened the door. "Cinnamon's here," he called out, gesturing her inside.

The aromas of roast beef and baking bread filled the air, making her mouth water. Fran strode into the room, her thick braid swishing over her shoulder just as it had five years ago. Shoeless, she wore a bright yellow *I Heart Dunlin Shores, Oregon* bib apron over a sweater and jeans. Her socks matched the apron. The love of bright colors hadn't changed either.

Even without shoes she stood a few inches taller than Cinnamon, who was exactly five-six—five-eight in the heeled boots she was wearing.

"Hey, you." Wearing the grin Cinnamon knew and loved, her eyes sparkling, Fran opened her arms.

It seemed ages since anyone had welcomed, let alone hugged, Cinnamon. Her eyes filled and she returned the embrace with equal warmth.

No tears, she sternly ordered herself. Crying was for pity parties, and hers was over. "It's so good to see you," she said, the words muffled in the hug. "Thanks for inviting me. I know you must be busy getting ready for Valentine Weekend—you're having a full house, right?—and the tourist season after that."

Fran pulled back to study her. "I am busy, but we'll have our evenings together. Don't worry, you'll find plenty to do during the day. I'm so glad you're here. Facetiming several days a week isn't enough." She sobered. "How're you doing?"

Cinnamon had plenty to discuss with her friend, but not in front of Nick. He had to have heard the concern in Fran's voice and noticed her troubled expression. "I'm managing," she said.

Her friend nodded. "Thanks for bringing that bag in, Nick. You two introduced yourselves, I assume?"

"We sure did." His voice was teasing and ripe with innuendo.

He showered Cinnamon with a long, slow look that made her forget her troubles. Her gaze flitted from his mesmerizing eyes to his chin, where a long, pale scar ran along his jaw, only noticeable in the bright light of the entry. Somehow it added to his attractiveness. Not that she was attracted. She was merely observing.

Ha.

She untied the belt of her raincoat and shrugged out of it. Or started to.

Nick set her suitcase down and helped, the perfect gentleman now—as if he sensed his effect on her.

For the second time she felt herself blush. He handed her the coat, his grin blooming again and the dimple winking. So full of himself. Not that different from Dwight.

She narrowed her eyes at him, but he'd already turned away to get her a hanger.

"I'll take your bags to the room and then I'm off," he announced, grabbing the suitcase, laptop, and toiletries case. He glanced at Fran. "The Orca Suite?"

"Right."

"That's on the third floor," Cinnamon recalled. A veteran planner, before arriving she'd studied the layout of the Oceanside posted on the website. "The Oceanside's only suite. According to the description, luxurious."

"You'd better believe it," Nick commented. "Private bath with a whirlpool tub big enough for two, a sitting room, fireplace, and a balcony overlooking the ocean. Takes up the whole floor. You'll like it." Whistling softly he headed up the carpeted staircase.

When he was out of sight, Fran leaned toward her. "Isn't he adorable?" she whispered.

"I was thinking more along the lines of hot and sexy. You never mentioned his looks."

"Oops. My bad."

"Well, he's not my type. Right now, no man is." Bruised feelings, dangerously close to the surface, threatened to spill out in a hot rush of tears. Not now, not now.

Cinnamon glanced around the brightly lit foyer and beyond to the blazing fire in the other room. "So that's the wonderful great room you rent out for weddings and parties. As I recall from the website, 'The main level's open floor plan allows guests easy access between the great room, dining room, and kitchen.' I can't wait to see everything."

Amusement twinkled in Fran's eyes. "You memorized that?"

"No, I pored over the website. That's known as attention to detail."

"Attention to detail." Her friend laughed. "That's so like you. And the reason you're such a good consultant."

"*Used* to be a good consultant, you mean."

The humor faded from Fran's expression. "You're still the best. We all make mistakes." There was no judgment or condemnation in the words or in her expression, only compassion and love. "Ease up on yourself."

Fresh tears filled Cinnamon's eyes. Jeez, she was sensitive tonight. She blinked furiously. "Can we please talk about something else?"

"Of course. How about a quick tour after Nick leaves?"

They both heard the thud of his footsteps on the carpeted stairs and his tuneless whistle.

"Speak of the devil," Fran quipped.

His lips quirking, Nick glanced from one woman to the other. "Are you two talking about me?"

By his confident stance and heavy-lidded eyes, he assumed he was the topic of conversation. "You wish,"

Cinnamon said.

"Ouch." Laying his hand over his heart he gave her a mock-wounded frown that lightened her mood a fraction.

"I'm sure you'll live."

"Thanks for taking the bags up, and thanks for your hard work today, Nick," Fran said. "See you tomorrow?"

"You bet." He saluted, his fingers flirting with his overlong hair. "As soon as I drop Abby at school."

He had a daughter. Probably a wife too, though Fran hadn't mentioned that. Yet here he was, flirting with her. Men! She gave him a dirty look, but he was focused on Fran.

"I have a dentist appointment first thing in the morning, and a long town council meeting after that, so I may not be around," Fran said. "Cinnamon will let you in."

"I'll look forward to that. You two have fun tonight. Don't do anything I wouldn't do, but if you do," he aimed yet another suggestive look at Cinnamon, "think of me."

Cocky, trite, and married. Cinnamon could hardly stand him, yet at the same time the attention felt really good. How pathetic was that?

In a blink his expression turned solemn and wary, as

if he understood she was an emotional wreck. She never had been good at hiding her feelings.

"What'd I do?" he asked, his contrite tone totally devoid of flirtation.

"It's not you," she said in a voice clogged with emotion.

His kind, sympathetic expression snapped her shaky control. She burst into tears.

Chapter Two

FEELING HELPLESS AND uncomfortable, Nick shifted from one foot to the other. He thought Cinnamon was cute in an uptight, corporate sort of way, and he'd enjoyed teasing her and making her cheeks flame. She was way out of his league, yet not immune to his attention. But then, flirting was one thing he knew he was good at.

Now the teasing was forgotten. Crying females made him nervous. They always had. Even his sister and niece. Abby took shameless advantage of the knowledge, and she was only twelve.

But Cinnamon wasn't trying to wheedle something out of him. Her bawling was genuine. His chest felt tight. He wished he could help, but she had plenty of smarts and an advanced degree in business, while he'd barely squeaked through high school.

A guy like him had nothing to offer her, and no business watching her fall apart. He looked longingly at the door, but unfortunately his escape was blocked by Fran and her sobbing friend.

"It'll all work out," she soothed, her arm around Cinnamon. "C'mon, let's go into the great room and sit down."

Cinnamon ducked under her grasp and visibly pulled herself together. She wiped her eyes and sniffled. "I'm fine now."

So she said. But tears continued to stream down her cheeks. She wasn't through crying yet.

Fran caught his eye. "There's a box of tissues in the powder room."

Nick nodded. On his way to the bathroom he passed the sliding-glass door along the wall of the dining room, which opened onto the deck. Beyond that were the kitchen and the basement stairs, leading to the garage with its door to the side yard.

He thought about sneaking out either exit, but Cinnamon needed those tissues. Retrieving the box, he returned to the great room, where a cozy fire crackled in the massive stone fireplace.

The two women sat side by side on the long sofa, their backs to him. He saw their reflection in the floor-to-ceiling ocean-view windows across the room, backlit by the tiny lights along the deck.

Cinnamon's head rested in her hands, her short, dark, spiky hair sticking up between her fingers. She wasn't crying anymore. Wasn't talking either. It was Fran's voice he heard, though she spoke so softly he couldn't make out the words.

He wondered what had happened to cause Cinnamon to break down in front of him. Whatever it was, he wanted no part of it. He'd hand over the tissues and leave. As he trudged reluctantly into the room the oven timer buzzed.

"That's the bread." Fran jumped up. "Excuse me." With a concerned look Cinnamon didn't see, she glanced at Nick and jerked her head toward the woman.

Trapped.

Sniffling, Cinnamon reached for the tissue box and blew her nose.

He backed toward the pair of armchairs catty-corner to the sofa. He didn't sit, because he wouldn't be here long enough for that.

Her red, swollen eyes met his, then skittered away, but he saw the bleak expression there. With the dark smudges of makeup on her cheeks she didn't look like an executive anymore. Not so pretty either.

Then why did he suddenly want to kiss her? Like that'd ever happen.

He stuffed his hands into his back pockets and cleared his throat. "Are you all through crying?"

She nodded and tried to smile but didn't quite make it. "I don't know what came over me. I've had a rough few months, and I guess they finally caught up with me."

The way she was looking up at him, he figured she expected him to say something. He shrugged. "I've had a few of those myself along the way."

"I'll bet you didn't cry though, did you?"

Inside he had—every time some kid called him a stupid moron. "I'm a guy. We aren't supposed to."

"Corporate vice presidents aren't either. Of course, now that I'm an ex-corporate vice president..." She laughed, a dry noise that sounded as if it hurt.

So she'd lost her high-level job. That must have really stung. He searched his mind for the right thing to say. "A woman like you should be able to find a new job fast."

She pulled in a shuddering breath, and for a moment he feared she'd cry again. To his relief she sat up straight and squared her shoulders. This time she looked squarely at him.

"Thanks for the vote of confidence."

Holding her head high allowed him a nice view of her long neck. He'd always liked necks, and hers was about perfect. Was her skin as smooth as it looked? He'd never know, and he had no business thinking that way.

What the hell was wrong with him?

He gave her a guarded look. "Need anything else?" She shook her head. "Then I'll be leaving."

He got out of there as fast as he could.

APPALLED AT HER temporary lapse of self-control—blubbering like a weak fool in front of a man she barely knew!—Cinnamon cringed on the sofa until the click of the front door signaled Nick's departure.

In her mind she saw his uncomfortable expression. He was so eager to get away from her he'd practically sprinted to the door. She released a groan of humiliation and smacked her forehead with the heel of her hand.

Rehashing and getting stressed over what had just happened would only make her feel worse. A better idea was to occupy her mind another way, by creating a to-do list for the rest of the evening and tomorrow.

All she needed was the notepad app on her smartphone. Unfortunately, she'd tucked it into the laptop bag Nick had taken upstairs. Emotionally exhausted and not ready to move, she settled for composing the list in her head, imagining the items arranged in chronological order.

First, tonight's tour of—

"The bread is cooling, the potatoes are simmering, and the roast is out of the oven," Fran announced. Frowning, she glanced around. "Did Nick leave?"

"A few minutes ago. I was about to come find you." Scooping the handful of used tissues from her lap, Cinnamon stood.

"Toss those into the fire. Are you feeling better now?"

With a sigh, Cinnamon wandered to the fireplace. "I'm drained and totally embarrassed, but yes, definitely better."

"I suspect you needed a good cry, and if you can't do that with your BFF…" Fran shrugged. "What I'm saying is, don't waste your energy feeling embarrassed."

"Nick isn't my best friend. I just met the man, and he saw me at my worst." Cinnamon lobbed the used tissues into the flames. Hissing, the yellow tendrils flared up, obliterating all traces of paper. If only she could wipe out her problems so easily.

"What he saw was a woman hurting—nothing to be ashamed of," Fran said.

"Mostly, my pride is hurt. Thanks to Dwight my life is in tatters, yet he walks away good as new."

"Which isn't fair at all. Be thankful it's behind you now. So are your tears tonight. How about a quick tour before dinner, ending at your room? I'm sure you want to freshen up." Fran pulled a screen in front of the hearth.

Cinnamon managed a smile. "Sounds good."

"This is the great room." Fran waved her hand toward the huge area, which aside from the big, comfortable furniture, was mostly floor-to-ceiling glass and open space.

"It's beautiful, perfect for parties." Cinnamon wandered to the chest-high bookcase separating the great and dining rooms, crammed with paperback books. "If I'd known about these, I wouldn't have brought my own stash. I can't wait to see the rest of the place."

"My apartment is in the basement. I'll show you later. If you need to do laundry, the washer and dryer are down there too. Let's start with this floor. This way to the dining room." She beckoned Cinnamon past the bookcase. "Even though I could eat in the kitchen and sometimes do, when there are no guests, I take my meals here in the dining room. When you get a look at the ocean view tomorrow morning, you'll understand." She squinted at the floor-to-ceiling windows and sliding glass doors. "Although the windows need a good washing.

Remind me to ask Nick about that."

The lights on the deck seemed to wink at Cinnamon. "He's a big flirt."

Her friend, who was headed for the kitchen, stopped and pivoted toward her. "Nothing wrong with a little harmless flirtation," she said, rotating the loaf of bread that was cooling on the counter. "You didn't seem to mind."

"I can't believe what I'm hearing. The man is married with a daughter. He shouldn't be flirting."

"Married?" Fran's jaw dropped. "Where in the world did you get an idea like that?" She entered the kitchen, Cinnamon following.

"When he mentioned his daughter. Where do you keep the glasses? I'm thirsty."

"In here." Fran opened a cabinet door. "Help yourself. Abby is his niece," she continued as Cinnamon chose a glass. "Her mom, who's Nick's older sister and a single mother, starts work at the cranberry factory, which I suggest you tour, at seven-thirty. She drops Abby at Nick's and he drives her to school. FYI, at the moment he's between girlfriends—single and definitely available."

Cinnamon didn't understand her relief at the news. She wandered to the sink. The window above it faced the same direction as the dining and great rooms. "After

Dwight, I guess I'm paranoid."

"Not all men are like that snake."

"You mean pursuing a subordinate—that would be me—while separated from his wife, convincing said subordinate that once the divorce came through, she was what he wanted, starting a sexual relationship, and then changing his mind and going back to his wife? Which forced the subordinate to resign? Gee, I hope not." No tears now. She was too angry at Dwight and her own foolish self to cry.

"You'll get past this."

"I'm halfway there already." She sounded a lot more convincing than she felt.

Fran moved to the stove and peered into a simmering pot, then turned her attention to Cinnamon. "Did you really love him?"

"I imagined I did at the time. Otherwise I never would have slept with him."

She couldn't ignore Fran's probing look. Knowing she was about to reveal an unflattering side of herself, she bit her lip. "Dwight Sabin is successful, sophisticated, well read, and fun to be with—qualities I look for in a husband.

"Not that I wanted to get married. I'd planned on waiting until I was at least thirty. But when he left his wife and pursued me, I was more than flattered. I changed my mind about marriage." She'd been such a fool. She paused for a sip of water. "I never realized how other people saw our relationship until it was too late."

The snide looks and comments, some from supposed friends, had stung. Babette Cousins, another vice president, had called her a "scheming bitch determined to sleep her way up the corporate ladder." Untrue, and so hurtful.

"I was so naïve." Cinnamon managed a laugh, flat and humorless as it was. "If I ever again mention dating a man separated from his wife, will you just shoot me?"

"I think you've learned your lesson." Fran opened the lower of her two ovens, nodded to herself and turned it off. "And I truly believe you're on the mend. That spicy undercurrent between you and Nick? I could actually feel the sparks—before you burst into tears."

Mortified, Cinnamon groaned. "Don't remind me. I'm not interested in Nick. When I decide to date again, the man I choose will be ambitious like me, and earn a big salary."

"That's your choice."

The slight edge to Fran's tone puzzled Cinnamon. "What's that supposed to mean?"

"Let me answer that with a question. Counting

Dwight, how many men have you been involved with over the past five years?"

"In actual relationships? Three."

Fran nodded. "All corporate climbers and all jerks. I see a definite pattern here, and I suggest you rethink the kind of man you want. There's more to life than ambition and money."

"You wouldn't say that if you'd grown up poor."

Cinnamon had. Her mother had never stayed with the same low-paying job for long. They'd lived hand to mouth, often moving in the dead of night to avoid paying the rent.

"But you earn more than enough to live the good life," Fran pointed out. "You don't need a man to depend on."

"No, but I want someone with the same ambitions and goals as me, a man who understands the importance of balancing a successful career with family. Anyway, for now I'm taking a break from dating."

"I don't blame you." Fran gestured beyond the kitchen. "If we want to finish our tour before dinner, we'd best get on with it."

Chapter Three

DURING NICK'S DRIVE toward Dunlin Shores Elementary School, grades K through eight, his usually talkative niece was quiet, her head bent over a math book. Serious and a perfectionist by nature, this morning she radiated tension.

A kid shouldn't be so uptight. He decided to lighten up her mood. As he rounded a bend in the winding road he gestured out the window. "Just look at that sky. Not a single cloud. If I didn't know better I'd think spring was around the corner instead of months away."

"Uh-huh." Abby didn't raise her head from the book.

At least she wasn't texting, but then, Sharon didn't let her take her phone to school. Braking at a four-way stop, he frowned and waited for the compact in front of them to go. "Don't you think you studied enough?"

She flipped her shoulder-length hair behind her ear, and Nick caught her worried look. "In case you forgot, the practice math bee is today."

"How could I, when that's all you talk about? It's only a warm-up, kid, so relax."

"I'm fine," she insisted, tightening her lips in the familiar way that reminded Nick of her mom.

He snorted. "The heck you are." The compact turned, and he headed forward. "You're so tense, you're about to snap. I can't imagine what you'll be like before the real math bee." Which was Friday morning, in Portland.

"Don't you get it? Even if this is a practice, I have to be the best." Her brow furrowed. "If I don't win, I won't get invited to the math camp in Virginia this summer. So puh-leeze let me study." Her attention returned to her book.

"Suit yourself." They finished the trip in silence.

Since third grade she'd been jabbering about the exclusive camp, a program designed for kids twelve through eighteen. Each age group competed for math bee state champion, and only the winners were allowed in.

Abby really wanted to go, and Nick figured she stood a strong chance. But winning a coveted invitation wasn't enough. The two-week program cost a bundle. A special math grant paid for the tuition, but room, board, and airfare were the responsibility of the family—in this case,

Nick. Sharon couldn't pay, not with her bills. As it was she had trouble scraping by. And with the cranberry factory up for sale and rumors of possible layoffs or worse...

He stopped himself. He wouldn't think about that, not with Abby in the car. Both he and Sharon had agreed there was no sense adding that worry to her already burdened young shoulders.

Her lips moved as she whispered to herself. She deserved to go to the camp with other kids like her. Who knew what could come out of that? Maybe a scholarship to college. Nick didn't have the smarts to go that route, but Abby did. She'd be the first person in the Mahoney family to attend and graduate from college.

Then, who knew? She might end up vice president of some corporation. Like Cinnamon. Except she'd lost her job.

For a January morning, the sunlight was unusually bright as it dappled the whitecaps. Nick reached for the sunglasses above the visor and thought about Cinnamon. He'd spent way too much time doing that, first on the drive home last night and later while lying in bed. After replacing gutters and working hard clearing dead brush from around Fran's foundation yesterday, he should have fallen asleep as soon as his head hit the pillow.

But no, he'd spent a frustrating few hours fantasizing a do-over with her crying friend. Massaging the strain from her shoulders as she poured out her troubles, then making her forget them in a very intimate way…

He stroked the steering wheel the same as he wanted to stroke and arouse her and started to get a little hot himself.

As if she'd ever want you.

Why would she? The women he dated didn't have advanced degrees. They laughed a lot, partied hard, and wanted what he wanted—good times and satisfying sex. The kind of relationships that never lasted long, but worked for him.

Cinnamon was smart, educated, classy, and as far out of his reach as the moon. Unless he wanted trouble and a bucket of pain, he'd best remember that.

"We're almost at school," he said, waiting for Abby to get her nose out of the math book. "I want you to listen to your uncle Nick."

She let out a sigh far too world weary for a twelve-year-old. "What?"

"You're going to ace the practice math bee and win the real thing," he stated as he neared the school. "I know it—" he thumped his chest "—in here."

Abby rolled her eyes. "You only feel that way 'cause

I'm your niece."

"I feel that way because you're the smartest kid in sixth grade, and the brainiest math whiz in the whole school. Just remember to relax. Your mind can't work right if you're too tense."

He knew this from personal experience. Give him time to puzzle out the words on a page and he could. Hurry him along and make him uptight, and the print looked as foreign as Arabic.

"How do I relax?" she asked, her forehead puckered.

"Simple. Take a deep breath." He drew in a breath and watched her do the same. "Now blow it out." They both did. "Tell yourself, 'I can handle this.' Then trust your brain and let it do its thing."

"Hey, that's pretty cool." His niece looked at him thoughtfully. "Where did you learn it?"

"From Mr. Edison, a high school teacher of mine."

The man who'd at last diagnosed Nick's learning problems as dyslexia, not mental retardation. At the time, Nick had been sixteen, still stuck in ninth grade and about to drop out. Mr. Edison had persuaded him to work hard and graduate. Four years later he had. His mother had died shortly after that, and he'd relocated to Dunlin Shores to start a new life.

Abby knew nothing about his reading problem. Nobody in Dunlin Shores did except Sharon, who'd followed him here eleven years ago. She'd promised to keep his secret, and had. In all those years she'd never brought up the subject. Neither had he, which was how he wanted things.

He shrugged at his niece. "What do you think? Gonna try it today?"

Her taut expression easing, she nodded. "Thanks, Uncle Nick."

When she closed her book and slipped it into her backpack, he gave a mental sigh of relief. Mission accomplished.

"How about I take you and your mom to Andie's tonight to celebrate?" The diner was a family favorite, and easy on the wallet.

"You mean if I win?"

"Have a little faith in yourself. Even if you don't win, you deserve a celebration for working so hard. And to keep up your strength for the real math bee." Signaling, he followed a school bus into the drop-off area. "Wish I could be there today to support you, but with the Valentine holiday coming up, Fran needs me."

The actual tourist season started at the beginning of April, but the days around February 14 drew plenty of couples eager for a romantic getaway. A few weeks after that, the tourist trade built and grew until the town hummed with visitors.

Nick was glad of the work. Fran wasn't his only customer, but she was one of his favorites. He liked her and she paid well. True, he'd prefer Cinnamon not be there, but if he stuck to a brief "hi" and focused on work, he'd be way too busy to think about her. He needed to stop at the lumberyard this morning, and might not even see her today.

In any case, she was only here two weeks. In that short amount of time he could put up with anything, even misplaced sexual desire.

"I understand, Uncle Nick—we need the money. As long as you come with Mom and me to Portland."

"Wouldn't miss that for the world," he vowed as he turned right. Even if it did mean leaving Thursday and driving four hours to get there, and precious money spent on a motel. Necessary tolls on Abby's road to success.

He braked to a stop at the drop-off area. School kids of all ages skipped and strolled toward the building's entrance.

"Have fun at Fran's, and tell her 'hi' from me." Abby opened the passenger door.

A year ago he would've tousled her hair, but she

didn't like that anymore. She was growing up way too fast.

He settled for a thumb's-up. " 'Bye, kid. Don't forget to breathe. Then knock 'em dead."

Her shoulders squared. "I will."

SHOWERED AND DRESSED, Cinnamon headed down the stairs. She could've slept in, but she was used to waking up early for work. She also wanted to have breakfast with Fran before her friend left for a dentist appointment.

Speaking of breakfast… The fragrant aromas of fresh-brewed coffee, frying bacon, and what smelled like muffins filled the air. Her mouth watering and badly in need of caffeine, Cinnamon hurried toward the kitchen. She heard her friend's voice. Who was she talking to?

Who else but Nick? He'd said he'd be here this morning.

But this early? Cinnamon faltered, then stopped outright. Maybe she'd sneak back to her room or take a beach walk before breakfast. Forget that. She had no reason to avoid Nick. She'd put on makeup and fixed her hair, the very actions bolstering her self-esteem. This morning she looked like her usual composed self, not at all emotional. No reason to mention her breakdown last night. She was good at pretending all was well, and had survived the last awful weeks at Sabin and Howe doing so.

In quick order she smoothed her cardigan twin sweater set over her hips, checked her hair, and pasted a smile on her face. Shoulders straight, she entered the kitchen.

To her surprise she saw only Fran. "Good morning," she greeted, glancing around with bewilderment. "I swear I heard you talking to someone."

"Hey, you." Dressed in a cheery red sweater and jeans covered by another bib apron, Fran stood at the stove over a skillet of sizzling bacon. "What you heard was my side of a conversation with Stubby and Stumpy, my seagull friends. They're not much for chitchat, but they're great listeners." She nodded toward the sliding glass door in the dining room. "They were sitting in their usual place on the railing, but flew off when they saw you."

For years Cinnamon had heard about the gulls Fran had "adopted," both with permanent injuries. She followed her friend's gaze, her attention stretching beyond the deck. The view, matched only by the view from her suite, was spectacular—sandy beach and an unobstructed vista of ocean beneath a clear blue sky.

"What an incredible view. The photos on your website don't do it justice."

"Didn't I tell you? We don't get many sunny days this time of year. Be sure you take advantage of the nice weather and get out on the beach."

"That's the plan. Do you think the gulls will come back? I really want to meet them."

"They haven't eaten yet. They'll hang around until I feed them. This is Wednesday, which means bacon. Extra crisp, or they throw fits. And the cheese-and-mushroom frittata had better be this side of piping hot."

Cinnamon laughed. "Sounds as if they have you wrapped around their little feet."

Amusement sparkled in Fran's eyes. "And they know it."

"I'm going to help myself to coffee." Cinnamon opened a cabinet stocked with cups, saucers, and mugs. "I thought sure you were talking to Nick."

"You should see the expression on your face. I don't care what you said last night. You're interested in him."

"I am not." Cinnamon chose a large mug emblazoned with two gulls soaring over the Oceanside Bed and Breakfast sign. "I meant what I said—I'm off men for a while. I'd rather avoid Nick."

"You're still wasting energy on what happened last

night?" Fran shook her head. "I'm sure he's forgotten the whole thing. Anyway, by the time he shows up you'll probably be out. He called a few minutes ago to let me know he was at the lumberyard outside town, picking up a few things. Could be another hour before he arrives. He'll be working on the deck today, replacing some rotted floorboards, but he needs access to the house, for the bathroom and so forth. So leave the sliding door unlocked."

"Will do." Cinnamon didn't understand the sharp prick of disappointment that followed. She wanted to steer clear of Nick, yet at the same time she hoped to see him.

Which was confusing, and not at all the way she ought to feel. She filled her mug. Regardless, she wouldn't be facing him today.

Chapter Four

"CAN I HELP with anything?" Cinnamon asked as Fran bustled around the kitchen. She wasn't used to being waited on. Even as a child, she'd been the one making breakfast for herself and her mother, who would've been content with coffee and cigarettes.

Fran shook her head. "I want to immerse you in the full guest experience. Except, I'm going to eat breakfast with you. I don't usually do that."

"You're sweet, but I'm not really a guest. I'm your best friend."

"Who insists on paying for her room, which makes you both."

"Yes, but you gave me a cheap rate. Way too low for a luxurious suite."

Fran waved off the words. "That's the off-season rate. So you like the suite."

"Who wouldn't love plush carpeting, a king-size bed covered with the softest sheets ever, and a fat down comforter? The cozy sitting room with the gas fireplace and the private balcony overlooking the ocean are unbelievable—as lovely as a suite at any four-star hotel," Cinnamon gushed. "This whole place is fabulous. I'm no small-town girl, but if I had an aunt Franny like yours and she left me this place... You're one lucky woman."

"Don't I know it. Even if you do prefer the hustle and bustle of big cities, you'll like Dunlin Shores. I wish I could spend all day showing you around, but with the Valentine's Day festivities almost upon us and me on the activities-planning committee, plus the meetings with the town council to keep them informed..." Fran shook her head. "Lately I'm so darn busy, it's not even funny."

Cinnamon stifled a pang of envy. "Don't worry about me. I have a to-do list myself."

Fran gave her a sharp look. "I thought you were here to relax."

Cinnamon didn't really know how to do that, but she intended to try. "I will, I promise. But I need a new job and I want to start looking. I sent out emails to colleagues in New York, San Francisco, and Minneapolis," she added, "and I want to follow up on their replies." Or would when she heard back.

"But this is supposed to be a vacation." The scolding tone was softened by Fran's concerned expression. "You haven't had one in years. Give yourself time away from the work world. You've earned that."

True enough. For the past five years Cinnamon had been too wrapped up in work to take off more than a few days here and there. But she enjoyed consulting, which added purpose and meaning to her life. Also, she hadn't saved as much as she should, and draining her savings was going to hurt.

"I can't enjoy myself with unemployment hanging over my head," she said. "But I do plan to spend a good chunk of time taking in the sights and getting to know the area. I'm planning to tour the cranberry factory this afternoon, after I walk the beach."

Fran brightened. "That'll be fun—and tasty, if you sample some of the products in the gift shop. Take your coffee into the dining room and let me finish this bacon. Oh, and help yourself to the cranberry juice. There's a pitcher on the table."

"No OJ?" Cinnamon made a face.

"I have it if you want it. But this is Dunlin Shores, Oregon. Our cranberry factory employs ten percent of our working population, and the chamber of commerce has asked all restaurants, motels, and bed-and-breakfasts to serve the juice every morning." Looking solemn, Fran lowered her voice. "Though to tell you the truth, the factory isn't doing well. It's been for sale for over a year with no takers. There are rumors that soon people will be laid off. The business may even close its doors for good. We'll be discussing the situation at this afternoon's town council meeting." She gave her head a dismal shake.

As a management consultant, Cinnamon earned her living working with businesses struggling to survive. From what Fran said, the factory could be on its last legs. "Sorry to hear that," she said. "Forget the OJ—I'll drink cranberry juice this morning."

She wandered into the dining room. With the table positioned in front of the sliding glass door, every seat commanded a view of the ocean. As soon as she settled into a chair, two scrappy seagulls, no doubt the pair Fran had adopted and spoiled, lit on the deck's wooden railing directly in her line of vision.

"Nice to meet you at last," she said, tipping her mug their direction.

Standing side by side, they watched her with cocked heads. Their beaks opened and closed as if they expected her to toss them treats. Through the window she heard their pleading shrieks.

"Begging, are you? Unless you drink coffee or cranberry juice, you're out of luck," she told them.

From the kitchen, Fran laughed. "Oh, they'll get

theirs."

As the birds blinked and hop-stepped along the railing like a pair of vaudeville comedians, Cinnamon couldn't help chuckling too. "They sure are entertaining. Which is which?"

Leaning across the counter that divided the kitchen and dining room, Fran peered at the beggars. "Stumpy's the one with no webbing on his foot. Stubby is holding up his left leg." She walked into the room with a half-dozen steaming blueberry muffins arranged in an attractive metal basket, then set it and a platter of still-sizzling bacon on the table.

The timer on the top oven buzzed. "There's the frittata," Fran said.

Seconds later she brought the egg dish into the dining room, setting off a frenzy outside. Both gulls flapped their wings and opened their beaks, making loud, demanding squawks.

"Patience, boys," Fran said. "There's plenty for you—after we finish." She shook out her napkin and placed it on her lap.

"We'd better eat fast," Cinnamon said. "No telling what they'll do if we take too long."

"They'll wait. *Bon appetit.*"

For several long moments they enjoyed the meal in

amiable silence. Such good food.

Far too soon Fran glanced at her watch. "If I want to make that dentist appointment on time, I'd best feed the birds and scoot. I'll be back late this afternoon. I thought we'd eat at Andie's Diner tonight, one of my favorite restaurants. The fridge is full of cold cuts. If you're here during lunch, help yourself. There's a spare house key hanging on the hook by the back door, and others in the catch-all drawer near the sink. Be sure to take one with you when you go out, in case Nick leaves before you get back and locks the slider."

"I'll clean up the kitchen," Cinnamon volunteered.

"I don't let guests do that, but I'll let you. Everything goes in the dishwasher." Fran piled the gulls' breakfast onto old plates, which she set on the deck. Car keys in hand, she waved as she headed down the basement steps. "Have a good time, and see you this afternoon."

A moment later the garage door squeaked open, squeaking again as it closed. Cinnamon waited for the gulls to devour their meal, then collected their empty plates and brought them inside. In no time she straightened up the kitchen. She phoned the cranberry factory and set up an afternoon tour, then returned to the dining room and enjoyed a leisurely second cup of coffee, a luxury she wasn't used to.

As relaxing as it was to stare at the view, doing nothing made her antsy. For years she'd rushed off to work at the crack of dawn. Now she was free and easy. And alone.

The gulls, who'd flown off a moment ago, returned to study her. She watched them with delight and tried to sit still. She felt too unsettled and at loose ends for that. Lost. Unemployed, no better than her mother.

A disturbing thought. Cinnamon stiffened. "I'm not like her," she told herself. "I want to work."

She decided to spend time online this morning and call a few colleagues. While she finished her coffee, she stared at the whitecaps dancing in the ocean. But the fluttery motion, or maybe the second cup of coffee, made her restless. The worry crept back. What if she couldn't find consulting work?

"Then I'll do something else," she stated, sick and tired of herself. Relax. Fran had left several brochures on the counter. Cinnamon decided to pore over those and figure out which places to visit during her stay here. Then she'd take that walk, which should help calm her down.

She spread the brochures on the table. Unlike larger cities, Dunlin Shores offered only a small art gallery and a limited number of cultural events. The whale watching looked interesting, but the company was closed till April. The game park was open, though, and it looked promising, as did the historical museum. Hmm…

Loud squawks jerked her attention outside. Wings flapping, the gulls soared away. Footsteps thudded on the deck, and Cinnamon's stomach flip-flopped.

Nick had arrived.

HIS BREATH VISIBLE in the chill air, Nick set a heavy blue tarp and circular saw on the deck. Late January wasn't the best time of year to replace the rotting floorboards, but with the Valentine's Day holiday in a few weeks, followed by a steadily growing parade of tourists that would last through late October, now seemed the best time.

For this job, he needed to bring a lot of equipment and supplies up here—the table he'd designed for his circular saw, the usual tools, nails, cedar tongue-and-groove planks, and the sawhorse. Hauling all that up the steps and a cup of hot coffee ought to keep him warm.

He drank gallons of the stuff, and Fran kept a pot ready for him. Blowing warmth into his icy hands, he headed for the slider off the dining room.

And saw Cinnamon scrambling up from the table.

She'd been watching him. Huh. He frowned. Wasn't she supposed to be gone by now, sightseeing or whatever? No big deal. He'd stick to his plan—say hello, refill his Thermos, and get to work.

After wiping his boots on the welcome mat, he slid the door open. "Morning."

"Hi." Without quite meeting his eyes she offered a flimsy smile.

Could she be any more tense? Nick remembered a similar forced expression on her face last night. He hoped to God she didn't start bawling.

She must've slept well. The fatigue had vanished from her face and her eyes were clear. No sign of tears either. *Phew.*

Without last night's unhappiness spoiling her features, she was more than pretty. A pale blue sweater set outlined her breasts, and her pants hinted at round hips and slender legs. "You look a lot better than you did last night."

Had he really said that? He shifted his weight. "What I mean is, you look rested and much happier."

The flush he liked rose to her cheeks. "I am, thanks. I don't usually break down like that," she went on, clasping her hands together as if she needed to hold on to something. "I'm hoping you forget that whole embarrassing thing."

"I'd forget my own name if it kept you from crying."

"I was that bad, huh?"

Her lips twitched, but he wanted a full grin. "I don't know—I can't remember."

Her mouth curved and widened as the smile he sought bloomed on her face. Beautiful. At last she looked straight at him. Sunlight from the window lit up her eyes. They were an unusual rust brown. Last night he hadn't noticed. "Is that how you got your name? From your cinnamon-color eyes?"

"That's right. Most people don't make the connection. Thea—that's my mother—couldn't decide what to name me. I was 'Baby Girl' until my eyes turned this color when I was around six months old."

"No kidding." Nick shook his head. "I've always been Nick, the same as my old man."

"I never knew mine. According to Thea he could have been any of several."

"I didn't have much of one, myself. Dear old Dad split when I was ten, and I haven't seen or heard from him since. Now Mom's gone too. Bad heart."

"I'm sorry to hear that."

"It was a while ago." He turned toward the kitchen. He meant to brush past her, but his arm grazed hers.

Although they both wore long sleeves, the touch jolted him. She must've felt the same strong current. Her eyes widened. They jerked away from each other. Nick started again for the kitchen.

"Did you want something?" she asked.

Oh, yeah, but nothing he cared to voice. He stopped and turned toward her, hooking his thumbs on his tool belt. "Do you?"

She glanced at his belt, then lower, before her gaze flew upward. "In the kitchen, I mean," she added, slightly breathless.

"Coffee. Fran keeps a pot for me."

"Help yourself." Her hands fidgeted with each other, and she gave a vigorous nod.

Nick eyed her. "Are you afraid of me?"

"Why would you think that?"

"The way you twist your hands together."

She stilled. "It's just… I don't really know you, and this feels a bit awkward."

"I'll be here for a while, so you may as well get used to me."

"I have plenty to keep me busy."

"Gonna check out the town?"

"That and a few work-related things."

He puzzled over that. "I thought you were on vacation."

"You sound like Fran. I'll tell you what I told her. I am on vacation, but as you know, I'm also unemployed. I can't find a new job without looking for one, can I?"

He'd hit a sore spot. "That makes sense. You should know that employment opportunities around here aren't the best."

"I'm not going to look here. I like big cities. I made a list of companies to contact."

"Smart."

"I'm a planner by nature. Every night before bed I make a list on my cell phone and rank-order it. In the morning I look it over, adding or changing the items— same as I've been doing for years."

"Years, huh." She was way too organized and structured for him. What was the word for that? Anal. But then, she was a whole lot smarter than he'd ever be. She'd probably have another high-level job in no time.

"If it's ranked five or less, it gets done, period," she added. "Lower ranked, less important tasks might get pushed to another day or forgotten altogether."

For a busy corporate executive, that made sense. Speaking of busy, it was time to get coffee and start work. "What's on your list for today?" he asked instead. He noted the brochures on the table. "Lined up any tours?"

She nodded. "The Tate Cranberry Factory at—" she pulled out her phone and called up the list "—one-thirty."

"Interesting place. My sister and most of my friends work there. What else?"

"A beach walk this morning. After the walk, I'll make those calls."

"The ones on your do-to list."

"That's right. How do you keep track of your life?"

He never relied on written lists, not even if he wrote them out himself. Too much chance of misreading and screwing up. He pointed to his head. "It's all in here."

"Aren't you afraid you'll forget something?"

"Nope."

Her mouth opened and she looked ready to pry more into his life. She'd already skated way too close to his reading problems. He glanced at the kitchen. "If I don't get my coffee and start work soon, I'll be here till midnight."

He started for the kitchen, then stopped and pivoted toward her. "What happens if something unexpected throws off your plans and keeps you from finishing the first five items on your list?"

"I'm a very organized person, Nick. If something

unplanned pops up, I work around it."

She sounded like a vice president or higher. With the slight upward thrust of her chin, the light of self-assurance in her eyes and the firm I'm in-control press of her full lips, she looked the part too. Even her graceful neck seemed corporate.

Smart, cool, beautiful, and way out of his league. How many times had he reminded himself of this, and why did he want to kiss her more than ever?

He wanted more than that, wanted her restless and eager under him, her control forgotten. Wanting in on the action, his cock stirred. Well, hell. He stifled a groan, or meant to. A soft, strangled sound wrenched from his throat.

Cinnamon's eyes widened but she didn't look away. Neither did he.

Her lips parted and her expression warmed. He recognized the signals, knew if he moved closer, leaned down, and kissed her, she wouldn't stop him. She'd kiss him back, maybe more.

But getting involved with her was dangerous. Crazy, even. Not an option. Clearing his throat, he backed away. "I'll get my coffee now. And you ought to take that beach walk."

"Right. I need to change my shoes and grab my jacket."

Nick didn't relax until she disappeared up the stairs. He'd avoided kissing her. Barely.

What had come over him? Whatever it was it wouldn't happen again.

Chapter Five

ON THE WAY back to the Oceanside, Cinnamon picked her way around jutting rocks, scattered drift-wood, and brittle sea grass. She'd paid a fortune for her leather gloves and they were classy, but they didn't keep her hands warm. Her icy fingers sought warmth in the pockets of her parka—thankfully, she'd packed that. Her toes and nose were numb, and despite a wool cap her ears ached. But the pale winter sunshine, brisk sea air, whipping wind, and whitecaps exhilarated her. That feeling alone was worth the physical discomfort.

Entertained by the waves, the birds wheeling over-head, and the beachside cottages standing well back from the ocean, she'd walked longer and farther than she'd planned. She was almost out of time to grab lunch before the tour at the cranberry factory.

She thought guiltily of her laptop, which she'd in-tended to put to use before the tour. No time for an online job search now. Later this afternoon or tonight, then.

When she reached the B and B, there was no sign of Nick's truck. Her spirits plummeted, which irked her no end. For heaven's sake, she didn't even like the man.

But she *was* attracted to him. This morning he'd teased and charmed her with his devilish grin, his heavy-lidded, bad-boy eyes warming her wherever they lit. And who could resist a man with a tool belt hanging on his narrow hips and a healthy bulge below.

He was also funny and sexy. No wonder she had the hots for him. And how.

Okay, maybe she did like him. But she was on a much-needed break from men. Even if she hadn't been, Nick wasn't the career-oriented, upwardly mobile, sophisticated male she wanted to share her life with.

Although he was single—a definite step up from Dwight.

Cinnamon braced for the familiar pain that usually accompanied thoughts of her ex. But with the sea at her back, the Oceanside before her, and the salty breeze against her face, the messy past seemed far away. To her relief, her heart continued to beat without aching. No knots in her stomach either. She owed Fran for suggesting she visit.

Despite being nearly out of time to change and eat

before the tour, she segued past the front door and around the far side of the deck. Unable to stop herself, she climbed the stairs. The blue tarp was still there, anchored by a large power saw on a worktable and neatly arranged tools. There was a large gaping hole in the floor where wood planks had been ripped off. Nick wasn't through, after all. She'd see him later this afternoon, a cheery thought that lifted her spirits way too high.

Unable to reach the slider, she headed back down the steps toward the front door. With fingers made clumsy from the cold, she fumbled the key into the lock, then opened the door and hurried inside.

The warmth of the house wrapped around her. She peeled off her gloves and checked her watch. If she didn't hurry, she'd be late. Better eat in the car so as not to miss the tour.

With so much to do, who had time to think about a man she had no business drooling over? She pushed Nick Mahoney from her mind.

"YOU'LL LOVE ANDIE'S Diner," Fran told Cinnamon as they ambled down the sidewalk, past cheerful streetlights and parked cars. "Great food at great prices—a favorite among the locals."

"I can hardly wait." Cinnamon's stomach growled. "Since I pulled into your driveway last night, it seems as if I'm always hungry. I could gain ten pounds without half trying."

"I hope you do," Fran said with her trademark bluntness. "You're too thin."

"Stress-related weight loss. Leaving the city and coming here was exactly what I needed. How did you know?"

"Lucky guess." Fran studied her with a caring eye. "I already see a difference in you. Even in the streetlights your healthy glow is obvious."

Only one thing dampened Cinnamon's upbeat mood—the uncompleted to-do list. She'd had every intention of starting her job search this afternoon, but after the factory tour and then an impromptu drive around town, she'd returned to the Oceanside scant minutes before Fran.

By then dusk had fallen, the hole in the deck floor had been repaired, and Nick had gone. A huge relief. Out of sight, out of mind. She hadn't thought about him once since she and Fran had headed downtown for dinner.

"It's a shame you're not here during tourist season when the shops stay open later," Fran said as they passed stores that had closed for the day. "They're fun to browse through."

"I'll come back tomorrow." After she looked for work.

The job search was crucial, a task she couldn't afford to put off. Yet today she'd done just that. The scary feeling in her gut threatened to ruin her appetite. Never mind, she'd start the search tonight before bed. Instant stress relief.

"That's Andie's." Fran pointed out the pink neon Andie's Diner sign at the end of the block.

Moments later they hung their coats on the over-loaded tree near the door. The fifties style diner was noisy and crowded. As they made their way toward a vacant booth halfway across the room, waitresses and customers called out greetings. A few even used Cinnamon's name, which surprised her.

"How do they know who I am?"

"We don't get a lot of visitors this time of year. That makes you big news."

"I'm not sure I like that," Cinnamon muttered.

"No one here bites, I swear."

They slid into a booth angled with a view to the door. Cinnamon sniffed the air, her mouth already watering. "Something sure smells good."

"Andie's home-cooked meals are top-notch. I highly

recommend tonight's special, whatever it is. Here comes the woman herself."

A short, wiry fiftyish waitress in support hose, clean white sneakers, and a hot-pink uniform that matched the neon sign appeared at the table bearing water glasses and napkin-wrapped silverware. She smiled at Fran. "Hey there, sugarberry." She turned her smile on Cinnamon. "You must be Cinnamon. Welcome to Dunlin Shores. I'm Andie."

Right off, Cinnamon liked the friendly woman. "I hear this is a great place to eat."

Without a trace of conceit, Andie nodded. "That's a fact. We use the finest ingredients and old family recipes handed down from my great-great grandmamma, Giulia Soldano. I can give you a menu, or you can trust me and order tonight's special."

"That's what I told her," Fran said. "What is it?"

"Spaghetti with clam sauce, garlic cheese bread, and green salad with house dressing. For dessert, cranberry pound cake with hot fudge sauce."

Fran licked her lips. "Yes please, and a cup of decaf."

"Make that two," Cinnamon chimed in.

The restaurant owner winked. "Smart girls. I'll be back with that coffee."

By the time Fran and Cinnamon unwrapped their

silverware, Andie had filled their mugs and moved to another table. Cinnamon sampled her coffee, which was strong and surprisingly good for decaf.

"How was the factory tour?" Fran asked as she doctored her drink with milk and sugar.

"Interesting. I learned all about cranberries and how the juice is processed. But the building and equipment are run-down, and the employees seem depressed. Such a shame."

"Don't get me started," Fran murmured. "You know that town council meeting that took up my afternoon? We spent a good part of it discussing that mess. We all agree, the downslide started eight years ago, when Randall Tate bought the business. Who knows why. The man lives in Chicago and owns a dozen companies headquartered in the Midwest.

"When he bought the factory and retail store, both facilities needed upgrades and new equipment. He never sank a dime into either. Today, bringing the place up to snuff would cost a fortune. Thanks to stiff competition, even if Tate did modernize, there's no guarantee of profits." She sighed. "No wonder nobody wants to buy the business."

"And if it doesn't sell?"

"The way things are going, the factory could close

within six months." Fran cupped her mug as if the warmth from it could ward off the chilling thought. "Imagine ten percent of the population—207 men and women—all searching for jobs in Dunlin Shores at the same time. Sure, tourism is strong here, but we can't absorb that kind of unemployment."

Wearing a grave expression Andie delivered the salads. "My business would suffer too, especially during the off season. I can't afford that. We have to do something to save the factory."

Fran nodded. "That's why the mayor and town council have called an emergency meeting next Tuesday at 7:00 p.m. The public is encouraged to attend, so spread the word."

Andie brightened. "Now, that's something I can do."

As she turned away, Fran gave Cinnamon a considering look. "You work with struggling businesses. Maybe you can help."

"That's my field, but the companies that hire me pay high fees for my expertise." At least, they had when she'd worked for Sabin and Howe. "Seems to me, if the Tate Corporation wanted to hire a consultant, they would have by now."

"I hadn't thought about the fees." Fran glanced at her plate. "Suddenly I've lost my appetite. You want my salad?"

"Skipping dinner won't solve anything," Cinnamon pointed out. "You don't want to drop weight like I did, and get too thin."

"I suppose you're right. Let's change the subject and talk about something else." Cinnamon's friend dug into her salad. "How about my newly repaired deck. Didn't Nick do a great job?"

She *would* mention him. Cinnamon focused on her salad. "I don't know anything about carpentry."

"In my book, the man is a genius. That deck is fifty years old, with a tongue-and-groove floor. Replacing the rotted wood with boards that match the original takes skill and a ton of work. Nick even fashioned a special saw blade to do the job right. He's also fast and thorough. I sound like a TV ad, huh? I'm lucky to have him. He doesn't mind doing nonskilled labor either. He's agreed to wash all the windows and prune the trees."

"When will that be?"

"Tomorrow. There's a ton to do before Valentine's Day, so he'll be at the B and B every day until he finishes. Don't worry, he won't bother you."

As if. Cinnamon was already bothered. Make that hot and bothered, like it or not. She was also curious. "Nick works for you, but what else does he do to earn his living?"

"I'm not his only customer. He can fix just about anything, and always has a job waiting. He's also good at making replacement parts for old machines when those parts are no longer available. He's patched up a machine or two at the cranberry factory, or so I hear."

"If he's that good, surely he can find full-time work."

"He's had offers. I don't think he wants to be tied down."

Cinnamon's mother had used that same excuse dozens of times to avoid working a regular job. Down that road lay poverty, a place Cinnamon had no intention of visiting ever again. Further reason to avoid Nick, no matter how attractive he was. "I couldn't live like that."

Fran shrugged. "He seems to have everything he needs."

The door opened, ushering in a blast of cold air Cinnamon felt halfway across the room. She glanced at the newcomers. A young girl in a turquoise parka and cream scarf entered, followed by a woman in her mid-thirties, whom she recognized from the factory. Behind the woman, Nick.

For once he wore a coat—a denim jacket that hugged his shoulders. His face was ruddy from the cold.

Her heart gave a joyful kick before Fran aimed a

canny stare her way. "Did you see who just walked in?"

"Yes, and don't look at me like that."

"Like what?" The tone was pure innocence.

As if he sensed Cinnamon staring, Nick looked straight at her. His eyes narrowed and he gave a terse nod. Apparently, he wasn't thrilled to see her either. He glanced at her lips, which she realized had parted on a dreamy sigh. She quickly compressed them. His gaze, now intense, met hers, not in flirtation, but something deeper and more dangerous.

The noise seemed to dim. He's not what I want, she reminded herself. Her body, already hot and hungry, refused to listen. She jerked her attention away and pushed the remains of her salad around the plate.

"They're coming this way," Fran said.

Pretending indifference, Cinnamon pasted a pleasant smile on her face. But inside, every cell in her body went on alert.

Chapter Six

IN THE DOORWAY of Andie's, Nick hesitated. He hadn't expected to run into Cinnamon. Yeah, he'd thought about her a lot today. Her corporate skills and that to-do list? Not his thing. Still, he was attracted to her. By the flare of pleasure lighting her eyes, the feeling was mutual.

"There's Fran," Abby said, pushing her hair behind her ears in a pint-size feminine gesture much like her mother's. "I can't wait to tell her about winning the practice math bee!"

She rushed forward, coltish legs skipping over the black-and-white linoleum.

Flushed with happiness over her daughter's win and exuberant mood, Sharon laughed as she and Nick followed at a more leisurely pace. They knew most everyone here, and their progress slowed as they stopped to exchange greetings.

He considered a casual nod toward Fran and Cinnamon, then finding a place to sit. But the diner was packed, and the only way to reach the lone empty booth was to pass by them. Abby was yammering away at them, and he figured they needed rescuing.

Wearing a neutral expression he joined his niece, standing between her and Sharon. Both Cinnamon and Fran were focused on the girl, allowing him to study Cinnamon without her knowing. Her color was a good deal healthier than this morning. Sun or windburn, he figured. A day in Dunlin Shores tended to put the roses in a person's cheeks.

By the amused gleam in her eyes, she enjoyed listening to Abby, whose excitement seemed to bubble out of her.

"It was just the practice bee," she was saying. "But I won!"

As she paused for breath, Nick chimed in. "As you can guess, she's real excited."

"And she should be." Fran grinned at her. "I'm so proud of you, Abby."

His niece beamed, and his heart seemed to swell in his chest. He was proud of her too, and seeing her happy felt good.

"You must be great at math." Cinnamon's smile crinkled the corners of her eyes. "That talent will take you far in life."

She seemed comfortable and at ease. Without the worry tightening her face, she looked younger and prettier than ever. Beautiful even. Forgetting himself, he drank her in, feeling as though he could watch her all night.

He stared until Sharon nudged him and he remembered his manners. Clearing his throat, he made the introductions. "This is Abby's mom and my sister Sharon. Meet Cinnamon, a friend of Fran's."

Cinnamon extended her hand the way she probably did all the time in the corporate world. "Pleased to meet you."

Nick's sister looked startled—people didn't often shake hands with her. She handled it without a hitch—a small thing, yet, judging by her newly confident expression, important.

"I saw you at the factory this afternoon," Sharon said. "I was the one in the shower cap, tending the sorter." She fingered the clip that held her shoulder-length hair back at the nape.

Cinnamon nodded. "I remember. I was impressed by how seriously you took your job."

"Thanks for noticing." For an instant Sharon stood taller. Then her shoulders sagged. "Although the way things are going lately, I don't think it matters much what I do there."

Had she forgotten their decision to keep the factory troubles from Abby? Nick sent his sister a warning frown and cocked his chin his niece's way. Sharon closed her mouth.

Oblivious to the exchange, Abby remained focused on Cinnamon, taking in her dark green sweater that looked expensive, the strand of pearls around her neck, and the pearl studs in her ears. In a word, she looked star struck. Sharon also seemed taken.

"Tomorrow night, my Mom, Uncle Nick, and I are driving to Portland," Abby chattered on. "We're staying at a motel and everything! Then Friday morning I compete in the real math bee." Her enthusiasm dimmed. "I hope I win."

Nick squeezed her thin shoulder. "You will, kid."

"I have a hunch your Uncle Nick is right on the money," Cinnamon said.

Her encouragement made him like her all the more, whether he wanted to or not. They'd said their hellos. Time to head to their own table. "Did you get all the stuff on your list done?" he asked instead.

The pinched, tense expression returned to her face, making him wished he hadn't asked. "Not yet, but I'll have plenty of time to search for job openings when I get back."

"You're out of work?" Sharon sighed with the sympathy of a woman soon to be in the same boat. "I didn't realize."

"Cinnamon is a talented woman," Fran said. "She'll find something soon."

"Of course I will," Cinnamon agreed, but her assured tone and raised chin didn't quite mask the underlying anxiety.

Any fool could see how worried she was, including Abby. Her own face sobered. "Miss Smith?"

"That sounds so formal. Please, call me Cinnamon."

"Cinnamon. My uncle Nick taught me how to relax so my mind can work and do what it needs to." Abby glanced up at him, her eyes shining. "That's how I won the practice math bee. You can try that when you look for a job."

"Thanks for the tip. Maybe next time I see him, he'll teach me."

Cinnamon's eyebrows arched in curiosity and something more. He wasn't sure, but he thought she admired him for helping Abby. He offered an aw-shucks shrug. "Sure."

"It's not hard at all, you just breathe and tell yourself

to stop worrying. It really works." Every part of his niece bounced up and down, even her hair. "You can teach her right now, Uncle Nick!"

Him, a man who struggled when he read, teach anything to Cinnamon, an educated executive? Not likely, unless she wanted to know how to fashion a machine part out of scrap. With her, Fran, Abby, and Sharon all staring at him, he felt awkward and out-of-place. He shoved his hands in his jeans pockets.

Andie showed up balancing two steaming plates. "Whatever Nick was going to teach you will have to wait—dinner has arrived," she announced as she placed the plates in front of Cinnamon and Fran. "And we all know this food tastes best while it's hot. Enjoy, girls."

Relieved, Nick gestured at the empty booth. "Let's grab that booth and let them eat in peace."

"Nice meeting you, Abby, and best of luck Friday," Cinnamon said. "Good to meet you too, Sharon."

His sister brightened with pleasure. "You're here for two weeks, right? I hope to see you again."

"I'd like that."

Nick gave his head a mental scratch. His single-mom, high-school-grad sister and the college-educated Cinnamon were as different as plastic and copper tubing, yet they seemed to like each other.

"See you tomorrow, Nick," Fran said. "Even if it ra—"

Andie silenced her with a no-nonsense look. "What'd I say about eating your food while it's hot?" She glanced meaningfully at Nick and Sharon. "I may as well take your orders now, but you gotta sit down first."

Nick could have kissed the restaurant owner for putting an end to the conversation. He slid into his seat in the booth. "What's the special tonight?"

HUNCHED AGAINST THE driving rain, toolbox tucked protectively under his arm, Nick took the Oceanside steps two at a time. No surprise that yesterday's sunshine had given way to the usual January rain. He wouldn't be tree pruning or washing windows today. Everyone knew he was driving Sharon and Abby to Portland later. He could have taken the morning off and stayed home, but Fran expected him.

Icy breath huffed from his lips, and despite dashing from the truck to the stairs, his hands were wet and cold. Under the shelter of the deck, he wiped his palms on the thighs of his jeans, then clomped across the deck to check his work from yesterday. The entire floor needed a power wash and a coat of sealer, but it'd do for now.

Yesterday morning Cinnamon had been sitting at the table, sipping coffee. As he swung toward the sliding doors, expectation made his heart thud from more than taking the stairs two at a time.

She wasn't there. Disappointment sluiced through him, as unwelcome as the icy water trickling down the back of his collar. Ignoring both, he checked the slider. Unlocked. He wiped his feet on the mat, then stepped inside. "Hello?"

"I'll be right there," Fran called out from the kitchen. Seconds later, she appeared with two steaming mugs. which she set on the dining room table. She wanted to start his day with friendly chitchat. He was okay with that.

"This is fresh-brewed and extra-strong, the way you like it," she said.

He set his toolbox on the floor, then took a seat in front of the coffee. Heat from the drink seeped into his fingers, and the fragrant steam warmed his nose. "It's a nasty one today."

"So I see." She sat down across from him. "I told Cinnamon to skip her morning run, but she insisted."

So that's where she was. Nick scoffed. "What is she, nuts?"

"Disciplined and stubborn. Since college, every

Tuesday, Thursday, and Saturday, rain, snow, or shine, she does her three miles." Fran glanced at her watch. "She left about ten minutes ago, heading for the road. I'm surprised you didn't see her."

Aside from a few vehicles cautiously picking their way through the driving rain, Nick had seen no one. "This is flu season, and with the cold and rain… What was she thinking?"

"Believe me, I tried to talk her out of this. Keeping to a schedule is as important to her as your toolbox is to you. She had a chaotic childhood, and I think order and schedules make her feel in control."

"Huh." Nick wasn't sure he understood, not if sticking to a schedule meant jogging in the freezing rain.

"That's one reason why resigning from Sabin and Howe has been so difficult for her," Fran continued. "The schedule she relied on for years no longer matters."

Nick frowned. "I thought she was laid off. Why would she resign? Was the company doing something illegal?"

"No. Dwight Sabin—" She cut herself off. "I promised Cinnamon I wouldn't talk about that. The story is hers to tell."

Nick wanted to know, but what had happened was none of his business. He fiddled with his mug, and for a moment the only sound was the battering rain.

"You heard about the emergency town council meeting a week from tonight?" Fran asked.

He nodded. "Sharon and I will be there. Do you think we'll be able to keep the factory from closing?"

"Not without outside help." Her face was as bleak as the gray day. "Cinnamon works with companies in trouble. She's saved more than a few from going under."

"No kidding." Hope stirred in Nick's chest. "Do you think she can help us?"

"I don't know. She doesn't come cheap, and I doubt the Tate company will pay."

Considering the company's refusal to spend money on much of anything so far, that was likely true. His spirits sank.

"I'm going to bring her to the meeting, though. You never know."

"You never do," he agreed, but he didn't expect anything.

Neither of them spoke, each lost in dismal thoughts. Nick never wanted to work at the factory—he didn't want to work for anybody but himself—but he couldn't imagine Dunlin Shores without it. Where would all the laid-off workers, Sharon and friends among them, find work? His sister might be forced to move away, taking

Abby with her.

Nick hated the thought, but he wouldn't follow them if they did. Dunlin Shores was his home and he intended to stay forever. He felt comfortable in the small town, liked knowing his neighbors well enough that if they got too close, he could tell them to shove off and know that if he needed them they'd still be around. But without Sharon and Abby…

Tired of thinking about what might happen, and suddenly antsy, he drained his mug. "I'm leaving early today, and I should get started. What do you want me to do?"

Fran's eyes widened as she too noted the time. "It's late, and I have a bajillion errands to run. You can't wash the outside windows, but how about the inside? I took the curtains down and loaded them into the car for dry-cleaning. Also, the upstairs hallway and bedrooms need paint touch-ups. The leftover paint is in the garage."

Nick shook his head. "That won't work—it's been a few years, and wall color changes as it ages. I'll get some paint chips from the wall in each room and ask the hardware store to match it."

"I hadn't thought of that," Fran mused. "You're a genius, Nick."

He shrugged off the words. He'd learned through

experience, was all. "Anything else?"

"The garage door squeaks when it opens and closes. And the ceiling fan in the Orca Suite isn't working, but it won't be used till summer, so there's no hurry on that."

"May as well do it today, if Cinnamon doesn't mind me in her room."

"I told her about the windows. She knows you'll be up there."

Even so, working in her bedroom seemed like a breach of privacy. "I'll check with her first." If she ever got back. He glanced out at the wind-whipped ocean. "You shouldn't have let her go."

"What was I supposed to do, handcuff her and tie her to the dining room table?"

An image of Cinnamon wearing skimpy lingerie, writhing seductively as she tried to work her way out of handcuffs filled his mind. He shifted in his seat. "You think she'll make it back all right?"

"I do, but if she's not back in another ten minutes…"

They both stood.

"I'll go out and find her, then bawl her out for sticking to a schedule that makes no sense."

Fran's mouth twitched. "I'd like to see that."

Chapter Seven

MOST MISERABLE THREE-MILE run ever. Thanks to soaking wet sneakers and slippery ground, Cinnamon's shins hurt, a dull ache that signaled shin splints. Yet, desperate to escape the freezing rain that pummeled her head, shoulders, and thighs, she managed to jog up the Oceanside's driveway in record time.

Nick's truck was parked beside her car. Her plan had been to shower and leave before he showed up, but he'd arrived earlier today than yesterday. Not everyone kept to a regular schedule.

No doubt with her wet hair and red face, she looked disastrous, even less put-together than the night they'd met. But there was nothing she could to about that now.

Spent but forcing one last, punishing push, she sprinted to the steps leading to the deck. Near the top riser she slipped on the slick surface, whacking her shin hard. Pain exploded in her lower leg.

"Dammit!" she howled. Tears filled her vision. Crying wouldn't help, and blinking furiously, she sank heavily onto the step, which was sheltered by the eaves. Teeth clenched, she gripped her thigh with the fingers of her soaked gloves, as if that would stem the agony. Of course it didn't. Neither did the cold seeping into her behind.

After a moment she mustered the courage to examine the injury. First, though, she divested her icy hands of the sodden gloves. Slowly and carefully—mustn't touch the shin—she inched the microfiber legging upward with stiff fingers. Despite her care, cold water dribbled over the tender skin, stinging as it connected with the bloody, two-inch gash.

Chilled and shivering, she moaned, the sound drowned out by the pounding rain. Blood trickled down her leg—better than the flood it might have been. Already the area around the injury was puffy and red, sure signs of the nasty bruise to come.

Shivers shook her and her teeth chattered. Pain or not, she couldn't sit here any longer or she'd freeze to death. She rolled her pant leg up to the knee. Clutching the railing, she hauled herself up. Dizzy from pain or maybe shock, she stood where she was and waited for her head to clear. Then, using the wood siding for support, she limped slowly toward the slider. Or tried. Putting her weight on the leg was unbearable.

Ten feet wasn't so far, but Cinnamon didn't think she could make it. Nothing to do but phone Nick. If only she had his number. Lowering herself to the planking, she scooted on her rear end toward the slider. Unable to stand, she leaned against the glass and pounded on it.

It seemed like forever before Nick slid the door open.

"About time you showed—" The scowl on his face disappeared. "What happened to you?"

"I hurt myself, and I can't get up."

Warm, strong hands caught her. Inside, he sat her on a chair. "I'll get you a towel." Moments later, the warm terrycloth wrapped around her. "Tell me."

She sighed, feeling ridiculous. "I should've used the front door instead of the steps. I slipped and banged the heck out of my shin. It hurts, but I'm sure I'm okay." She tried to summon a smile of reassurance but couldn't manage it through her chattering teeth.

"My God, you're freezing." Grim-faced, he pulled the towel away. "Take that jacket off."

She wanted to, only her fingers were too numb. Nudging her hands aside, he unzipped the waterproof—*ha*—windbreaker and peeled it off. The long-sleeved tee underneath was nearly as wet.

"Soaked clean through," he muttered. "What the hell were you thinking, going running today?"

"I needed the exercise—"

"What you need is a dose of common sense. And you, with all that education. You got a bathrobe in your room? Because you can't stay in that shirt." He glanced at her sopped leggings. "Or those pants."

The disapproving tone chafed. Cinnamon struggled to stand, but Nick gently but firmly pushed her back down.

Who was this bossy male? She scowled up at him. "I want to take my shower now, so please—"

"Stay put." A glance at her shin and he shook his head. "I don't want you catching a cold and blaming me. I'll be back with your robe." He started up the stairs.

No one had ever taken care of her. For as long as she could remember, she'd looked after herself as well as her mother. Used to being in charge, she wasn't sure she liked Nick in that role. "Once I shower and warm up I'll be fine," she insisted.

"I'll be the judge of that. Don't move."

His gaze held her as sure as hands, and she nodded. "Okay."

The moment he disappeared she glanced at her chest. Wouldn't you know, her sports bra did nothing to conceal her cold nipples against her wet shirt.

Mortified, she crossed her arms, but of course, he wasn't there. Forget the robe and meekly waiting for him to come back. She'd dry herself off and head upstairs under her own steam, even if she had to hop on one leg to do it.

CINNAMON TOWELED HER hair dry, then set to work removing her shoes and wet socks, but her fingers were still numb and clumsy, and the socks didn't want to come off. She was still working on it when Nick returned with her robe, a formless navy flannel knee-length thing she wore when no one else was around. Too bad she hadn't brought her sexy satin robe instead.

Right. As if she'd wear that in front of Nick. Not that she wanted to model the shapeless robe for him either.

"I'll put on the robe later. I'm going upstairs."

"Are you nuts?" His jaw tightened. "You need to warm up."

"I can do that in the suite." Using one hand to hug the now-damp towel to her chest, she grasped the chairback with the other and pulled herself up. But the pain was overwhelming, and still hugging the towel to her breasts, she sank back down.

"That's better."

Nothing to do but change into the robe. Cinnamon held out her free hand. "I'll take that, thanks."

"All wet? Uh-uh." Holding the garment out of reach, he nodded at the towel. "First, strip off those dripping clothes."

"Excuse me?"

He released an exasperated breath. "I'll turn my back, okay? Just get out of those things."

Wearing a stubborn expression with his feet planted firmly in front of her, she knew he wouldn't budge until she complied. "All right."

"She finally comes to her senses." He tossed the robe onto the chair beside her, then faced the opposite direction.

"Close your eyes."

"What for? I can't see out of the back of my head."

"Close them anyway."

"Brother," he grumbled, and let out a muttered string of words she couldn't decipher. "All right, they're shut tight."

Acutely aware of his presence, she tugged the soaked shirt over her head. Her wet bra followed, both dropping onto the floor. How was she supposed to take off her jogging shorts and the leggings under them, when she wasn't standing up? She tried lifting one hip but that didn't work. Even the movement caused excruciating pain. A taut breath hissed from her lips.

"Cinnamon?" Nick started to turn around.

"Don't you dare move, Nick Mahoney. I'm half-naked!"

Uttering a strangled sound, he froze. "Are you or are you not all right?"

He sounded angry, which puzzled her. "No. I can't take my pants off sitting down."

"I suppose you want me to do it," he grumbled.

The thought of Nick helping with something so intimate emptied her brain of a reply.

"I'll take your silence as a yes." He sounded even more exasperated. "I won't turn around till you put on your robe."

"Good." She slipped into the flannel robe and tied the sash. The fabric felt warm, soft and unbelievably sensual against her cold nipples.

"Is it safe to turn around now?"

"One second," she said, hastily pulling the lapels together. "I'm ready."

As soon as he faced her his gaze dropped to her mouth, then to her hand at the vee of her robe. Without a word, he hunkered down in front of her.

Under different circumstances a man at her feet would have been romantic and suggestive. Wet, unwashed, and probably reeking, she was anything but attractive. Nick probably wondered how he was stuck sharing yet another mortifying moment of her life.

"Put your hands on my shoulders," he said.

He was wearing a black T-shirt, not much protection against the dead of winter. Yet under her cold hands he felt warm and solid, his strength honed from hard, physical labor. Not much fat on this man.

He reached for the waistband of her shorts and started to tug down. Cinnamon tensed. "Be careful of my shin."

Hesitating, he glanced up at her. "If I hurt you, tell me."

She nodded. He stripped off the shorts. "That didn't hurt at all," she said, surprised and relieved. But she worried about the leggings. His fingers hooked inside the leggings waistband and bikini panties. "Um, I'll keep my panties on," she said, feeling awkward and embarrassed by her helplessness.

"And here I thought I was about to get you totally naked." For the first time, his mouth quirked, a cockeyed grin that softened the moment. "Ready?"

Cinnamon nodded. For a big man he was surprisingly gentle. As he coaxed the reluctant fabric down her thighs and somehow cleared her injured shin, his muscles bunched under her palms. The clean smells of soap and man filled her senses.

Despite her throbbing shin the rest of her jolted to life, her need for Nick almost overpowering. She barely managed to keep from tangling her fingers through his dark hair, pulling his head up, and kissing him.

After what seemed decades, the leggings pooled at her feet. Tightening her grip on Nick's shoulders she lifted her injured leg while he carefully freed her foot from it. As soon as he took care of the other foot she let go of him and sank down. "I'm glad that's over."

"We're not done yet." Still hunkered at her feet, he held out his hand. "Let's see that shin." He cupped her foot in his warm, callused hand and studied her injury. "Ouch," he said. "You might have broken something. You probably need stitches too."

He released her foot. Instantly, she missed his warmth.

"I don't think so," Cinnamon said, hoping she was right. "The cut isn't deep, and the rest is just a bad bruise."

"You should see a doctor."

Which would put a bigger dent in her carefully planned day. "What I need is a shower, a cup of hot coffee, and my laptop."

He looked at her like she'd lost her mind. "Laptop?"

"I haven't made much progress looking for a job. I started, but it's slow-going."

Last night she'd found replies from exactly two of the many colleagues she'd emailed. Neither knew of any openings or leads. Cinnamon was beginning to think the rest of those she'd contacted weren't going to reply at all.

Which shouldn't surprise her. In the consulting community word traveled fast. It was likely that people had heard about her forced resignation and drawn the same unflattering conclusion as her coworkers.

Discouraged and exhausted, she'd collapsed in bed with hopes of a better attitude today. "I need to do more. I was also planning to browse some of the shops later."

"Plans change. You can take that shower, but if you want coffee you'll drink it in the car on the way to Doc Bartlett's. You're going, period."

Cinnamon rolled her eyes, which only tightened Nick's determined expression. "Who appointed you my keeper?"

"Someone needed to step up."

"If your Dr. Bartlett is like most doctors he's probably booked weeks in advance," she argued. "I can't just barge in."

"At Doc's, you can. I'll help you upstairs," he said. "While you clean up, I'll make that appointment."

"If you must."

His arm circled her waist and he helped her stand. He held on tight, and they made their way to the stairs. Cinnamon tried to hold herself aloof, but cradled in his solid warmth, she changed her mind and leaned into him. They started up the stairs. He was practically carrying her. Her head settled in the comfortable indentation where his arm and shoulder met, and she let out a sigh. She felt small and wonderfully coddled—a thought that stiffened her posture.

As soon as she tensed, Nick stilled. "It's no problem for me to pick you up and carry you the rest of the way."

Because the idea appealed to her, she frowned and tried to pull out of his grasp. "I don't need your help."

His arm remained around her waist. "Too bad—I'm not going away."

Chapter Eight

SQUINTING THROUGH GOLD-RIMMED bifocals, Doc Bartlett considered the X-ray that hung on the wall of the exam room. Nick stayed at Cinnamon's side at the exam table, where she sat with her legs outstretched, and also scrutinized the image. Not that he knew what he was looking at, other than her lower leg.

He doubted she knew either, although she studied the thing with the same intensity as Doc. Though unlike the unflappable doctor, tension pinched her mouth and fine lines creased the smooth space between her brows. Even her hands looked anxious, pleating her skirt. He figured she was scared, and with her legs bare, maybe cold.

Not the best way to dress in the winter, but better than cutting the leg off a pair of pricey pants or designer jeans. The skirt showed off her slender, shapely legs, and Nick appreciated the view—except for the angry-looking wound in the center of her shin.

The sight made his gut hurt. He wished he could comfort her, something he'd tried when Doc had cleaned the wound. Cinnamon had cried out and gripped Nick's hand with a surprising amount of strength. The minute the job was done, she'd let go and had balled her hands into white-knuckled fists, proving that he didn't know beans about soothing her.

Playing nursemaid never had been his strong suit. Anyway, he was only here because she was in too much pain to drive and needed the ride.

Which was a load of crap. He wanted to be here with her, even if it meant spending a long time in Doc's office. The beautiful, competent Cinnamon Smith needed him, and the novelty of that had sucked the marrow right out of his resolve.

The wet T-shirt under her worthless windbreaker hadn't helped either. One look at those taut nipples had stirred him up something awful. Stripping off her leggings was no picnic either. If that wasn't enough, knowing she was topless under her robe and wearing only the tiny panties he'd glimpsed had about killed him.

Dog that he was, he'd wanted her, bloody shin and all. That hadn't changed over the past hour. He'd best keep his eyes and hands to himself. As soon as the thought formed, her gaze snagged him, her big eyes telegraphing unease. Forgetting his newly made resolve, he reached for her, just as Doc pointed at the X-ray.

"What's the verdict?" Nick asked, his hand on her shoulder. She was smaller and more fine-boned than she looked.

If Doc had had a beard and a red suit, he could pass for Santa Claus. He smiled. "You're lucky, Cinnamon. Nothing's broken, and there are no hairline fractures."

"That's good news." Cinnamon released a sigh of relief.

So did Nick. She wouldn't need a cast. He'd take her back to the Oceanside, help her get settled, and then start on his chores. Too bad he had to leave early—he wouldn't get much done.

Holding her skirt in place with one hand she swung her legs over the table, wincing as she moved.

"Where do you think you're going?" Doc asked, his kindly face now as stern as a judge during a trial.

"I can't leave?"

"Not till I stitch up that gash." He frowned at the gaping wound, which had started to bleed again.

The color drained from Cinnamon's face. "Do I really need that?"

"Unless you want a scar."

Nobody asked, but in Nick's opinion, no scar could

ruin her leg.

"I don't. It's just, it hurts when anything touches it." Her hands started a fresh round of fidgeting. "The thought of stitches…" The words trailed off, and Nick feared she might pass out.

Doc gave a sympathetic nod. "I can give you something for the pain."

"And I'll hold your hand again, if you promise not to break my fingers," Nick teased, looking to coax a smile from her pinched lips. No such luck.

"I think I can handle this on my own." As pale as she was, she straightened her shoulders with grim determination.

She no longer needed him. Damn, that stung. At the same time, he admired her independence and strength. "Do you want me to step outside?"

"I would if I were you," she muttered. "I'm ready, Dr. Bartlett."

"I'll be in the waiting room." Silently wishing her luck, Nick wandered past two exam rooms, both occupied by patients ready for Doc, and returned to the check-in area.

This morning there were only two adults in the room, no surprise, as nowadays most people used the clinic outside town. Nick preferred the family doctor who'd seen him, Sharon, and Abby through injuries and all the childhood stuff his niece had caught and shared with them. Doc's friendly manner put Nick at ease. He also appreciated the convenient location.

What he didn't appreciate was seeing Liz Jessup on the sofa near the fish tank. As always, she was decked out in seductive clothes, this time a low-cut, clingy sweater, a short skirt, diamond-patterned hose, and heels so high he wondered how she walked in them. More suited to a club or bar than a visit to the doctor's office.

A guy couldn't help noticing her big breasts and round behind, but she wasn't Nick's type. Years back, the then thirty-something divorcée and single mom had hired him to fix her washing machine. Though he was ten-plus years her junior, she'd propositioned him more than once. He'd turned her down every time. Plenty of other men were interested, and she had her pick of dates. Word was, she wanted a husband, but so far no man had gone there. In the meantime she'd never stopped trying to seduce Nick.

Careful to keep his eyes off her impressive cleavage, he bypassed the sofa and took the chair next to Bill Patterson, a whale-size man who'd retired from the cranberry factory several years earlier.

"Morning." He nodded to both of them.

"Morning," Bill returned, hooking his thumbs through his trademark cranberry-red suspenders.

Liz fluttered lashes so long and black they had to be fakes, tossed her thick, wavy hair, and curved her red lips into a smile. "Well, hello, there." She crossed her legs, a move that revealed a long slice of thigh. "What are you doing here? I hope Abby's not sick, not with that math bee tomorrow."

Her legs were nice, but nothing like Cinnamon's.

Nick explained about the accident, while Bill, Liz, and Audrey Eames, the plump, gray-haired receptionist-nurse behind the check-in station, listened attentively.

"I heard Cinnamon was at Andie's last night," Liz commented. "What's she like?"

Bill nodded that he too wondered. "The one night I decided to eat in," he muttered.

Their interest came as no surprise. Winters in Dunlin Shores were dark, slow times, and they were curious about the only outsider in town.

"She's okay," Nick hedged.

Understatement of the year. Try sexy and beautiful, and about the classiest woman he'd ever met. Totally out of his league.

"That doesn't tell us much." Liz shook her head. "Men."

"She'll be through in a little while. You can see for yourself then."

"I met her when she checked in," Audrey said.

"Yeah?" Patting the cushion, Liz gestured her over. "Tell us about her before she comes out."

"Sure, for a minute." Audrey left her station, talking as she joined them. "She's a pretty little thing, slender, average height. Huge eyes and a spiky hairstyle that suits her."

Liz nodded, then glanced from man to man. "That's the kind of stuff we women want to hear about. What do you know about her as a person?"

At Nick's blank look, Bill shook his head. "Better tell 'em something or they'll nag you to death."

Nick shrugged. "I don't know that much, except that she's a former corporate executive looking for work."

"And she thinks she'll find it here?" Audrey scoffed. "Not with the cranberry factory in trouble."

"Big trouble," Liz seconded with a worried frown. Both her brother and her nineteen-year-old son worked there, one in shipping and the other in processing.

"Cinnamon isn't looking for work here," Nick said. "She came to visit Fran. They're old friends." He eyed Audrey. "Satisfied?"

"I guess I'll have to be."

The phone rang, and Audrey hurried back to her station.

In no mood for further conversation, Nick picked up a magazine and opened it, beyond caring that he couldn't read it.

Cupping Cinnamon's elbow, Doc slowly walked her into the waiting room. "She's all yours, Nick."

Ignoring curious looks from Liz and Bill, he tossed aside the magazine and stood.

"Be sure to ice that shin three times a day," Doc said, handing her an icepack. "If you change your mind about crutches or that pain medication, call me."

As Nick moved to her side, Audrey bustled off to ready the room for another patient. " 'Bye, Cinnamon," she called out in a pleasant voice. "I hope I'll see you again, only not here."

"Definitely not here," Cinnamon replied.

Nick grasped her arm as Doc had, but she brushed him off. "I want to do this by myself."

All right, then. He held up his hands. "Suit yourself."

"What were you reading?" she asked, shooting a curious glance at the magazine he'd tossed aside.

"Nothing." He jerked his chin toward the door.

"Let's go."

Cinnamon squinted at the magazine. "*Entrepreneur.* I read that issue a few months back. Did you see the article on building up your—"

"Liz, your room is ready," Audrey called from the hall.

"Be right there." The divorcée stood and sashayed toward Cinnamon. "I'm Liz Jessup, an old friend of Nick's."

She winked at him as if they shared a secret, and blew him a kiss. Nick pretended not to notice.

Ignoring the rebuff, she smiled at Cinnamon, who extended her hand the same as she had with Sharon. "Pleased to meet you."

"Likewise. I manage a store called Cranberries-to-Go, at the far end of Main Street. Be sure to stop in."

"I noticed your shop, and had planned to come in this afternoon." She glanced at the rectangular bandage covering her shin and offered a wry smile. "Not anymore."

"Too bad. Sorry about your accident."

"I should be fine by tomorrow. I'll come in then."

Nick doubted that. Unless her leg felt a whole lot better she wouldn't be driving anyplace for a while. He wouldn't be around to help her tomorrow either, as he'd be in Portland, rooting for Abby at the math bee. Fran would have to chauffeur her.

"I don't want to keep Doc waiting," Liz said. "I'll watch for you tomorrow, Cinnamon." She waved her scarlet nails at Bill, then blew Nick another kiss. " 'Bye." With a seductive sway of her hips, she strutted toward the exam rooms.

"She's pretty, in a dancehall-girl way," Cinnamon noted, shooting him a look he couldn't decipher.

He shrugged. "I guess."

From his seat, Bill cleared his throat. "I'm Bill Patterson. I'd get up but I had hip surgery awhile back and the darn thing's still stiff as a piece of driftwood."

Cinnamon gave him a sympathetic expression. "I hope it feels better soon. I'd come over and shake your hand but…" She glanced at her leg.

"Aren't we a mismatched set." If Bill's grin grew any wider his mouth would split, a sign that Cinnamon had charmed him. He glanced at her shin. "What'd Doc do to you?"

"X-ray and stitches, but they're the dissolving kind, so I don't have to come back."

"Lucky you. I had stitches, too. Mine itched like a son of a gun. Don't scratch 'em or you might need new ones."

"I'll remember that."

At this rate they'd never leave. Nick cleared his throat. "Can we go?"

Cinnamon's eyes widened. "Right away. 'Bye, Bill."

"Hope to see you again. Good luck finding a job."

Her startled gaze darted to Nick. This time she was easy to read, and he noted her displeasure with surprise of his own. What was the big deal? Her unemployment was no secret. He shuttled her out.

Chapter Nine

WALKING UNASSISTED OUT of the doctor's office required using the wall as a support. An awkward, cumbersome effort that took all Cinnamon's focus. To her relief, Nick let her be. She'd already leaned on him way too much. Bad enough he'd been forced to half undress her and then been stuck driving her here and waiting through the X-ray and stitches. In the exam room, she'd squeezed the life from his fingers like a helpless little thing, a maneuver her mother might've stooped to.

The thought made Cinnamon cringe. She detested weakness, had spent her whole adult life suppressing anything that resembled it. Yet this was the second time in a few days that Nick had seen her at her most vulnerable. He must think her an emotional wreck.

He held the exit open. Outside, she grasped the railing along the walkway and limped forward. The driving rain had turned into a cold mist that bit at her face and legs despite the large overhang that sheltered the area. Shivering, she pulled her jacket close.

"Cold?" He slanted her the same concerned look she'd seen earlier. She nodded. "If I had my jacket, I'd give it to you. You'll warm up in the truck." He glanced at the vehicle parked some thirty feet away. "Wait here. I'll bring it around like I did before."

His long legs rapidly covered the distance. He moved with an easy grace that made watching him a pleasure. Like all trucks, his required a big step to reach the cab. He climbed up and hopped into his seat. A moment later the engine purred to life.

Parking at the curb, he leaned over and opened the passenger door. He raised his eyebrows, silently asking if she wanted help. On the way here, he'd lifted her up and settled her in the passenger seat. But now that she was stitched up... She'd managed to make it through that, and she could manage this. She compressed her lips and shook her head, and he stayed in his seat.

For all her bravado, she couldn't bear much weight on her leg. She hobbled around the front of the truck, using the hood for support despite its being wet. And questioned her stubbornness. Just what was she trying to prove?

As she reached the passenger door, she hesitated.

She'd never get into her seat without more help from Nick.

"Are you going to yell at me if I give you a hand?" he asked with a wary look.

Had she sounded that bad? "I'll behave, I promise."

"Stand tight." He slid nimbly out of his seat. Seconds later he stood at her side. "Ready?"

She nodded. Warm hands grasped her waist. Though she weighed 115 pounds, he lifted her as if she were as light as her laptop. She held onto his solid biceps and felt his muscles flex. So different from Dwight's flabby arms.

"This isn't so bad, is it?" he said.

Was he kidding? She wanted him to hold onto her forever, "I'm handling it," she said, her voice not quite steady.

Heat flared in his eyes, throwing her body into chaos. He set her in the seat, his hands lingering on her waist longer than necessary. She itched to pull him close for a kiss and almost did. Then she remembered Liz's intimate smile at him.

Whatever the two of them had shared, sex was likely included. Hot sex. None of Cinnamon's business, but the very thought put a sour taste in her mouth. "You can let go now," she said, giving him a dirty look.

He released her, shut the door, and headed around

the truck. Cinnamon fastened her seat belt.

In the cab, he shook his head. "I don't get you at all. One minute you're friendly, the next, you freeze me out. What kind of game are you playing?"

"You're the one playing games. If you're involved with Liz, why are you flirting with me?"

"Dating Li—Are you joking?" Snorting, Nick buckled up. "Her son, Bret, is nineteen, only thirteen years younger than I am. She's too old for me, and she's not my type."

"Oh." Relieved and at the same time feeling foolish, Cinnamon sat back. "What is your type?" She could have bitten her tongue.

Smiling, Nick pulled away from the curb. "I like women who want to have fun, no strings attached."

"The same as Liz."

"That's all show. She's husband hunting and will do about anything to snag herself one. So far nobody's been fool enough to take the bait." As he waited for several cars to pass, he eyed Cinnamon. "What kind of man do you like?"

"He has to be single, upwardly mobile, financially comfortable, and interested in settling down and starting a family."

Stating her requirements aloud reminded her that

Nick wasn't what she wanted. Except, he had been reading that business magazine in the doctor's waiting room, which could mean he was more success oriented than she'd guessed.

She waited until he turned out of the parking lot to pose her question. "Did you happen to read the article in Entrepreneur about building your business?"

"No." His grip on the wheel tightened and his expression shuttered closed.

And he thought she was difficult to read. "Did I somehow offend you?"

"No." Now his whole body was stiff and tense, and a tiny muscle jumped in his jaw.

"Are you sure? Because suddenly you seem really uptight."

"Leave it." He turned on the radio and cranked up the sound.

Country music wasn't Cinnamon's favorite, especially when played so loud the whole truck vibrated. Bracing for an explosion, she cautiously turned down the volume.

None came, although tension continued to radiate from him. She sank against the seat. The rest of the drive back, neither she nor Nick spoke. Staring out the window at the modest houses and tree limbs dripping with rain, she mulled over the conversation and tried to figure out what had gone wrong.

Clearly she'd hit a sore spot about his handyman business, though what it could be eluded her. Fran said he was happy with less than full-time work. If he wasn't interested in growing his business, why not just say so?

No, she decided, his strong negative reaction stemmed from something else he didn't want to share. Which really wasn't her concern. She had troubles of her own. Still, she was curious.

She stole a glance at him, noting the taught line of his shoulders and the rigid clamp of his jaw—nonverbal barriers that warned her not to broach the subject again. Or any subject, for that matter.

By the time he pulled into the Oceanside driveway, she could hardly wait to get out of his space. Silent and sullen, he seemed to feel the same way.

Careful not to push any more hot buttons, whatever they might be, she let him help her down from the truck and escort her to the building, making small talk about the weather and Fran's seagulls. In the kitchen he made her a sandwich for later, found her a bottle of water, and filled the ice pack for her shin. Polite but distant, he handed her the items and helped her up the stairs. He had a ton of work today, and due to her accident, little time to get it done.

Equally polite, she managed a smile at the door to her suite. "Thanks so much for everything you did for me today. Tell Abby I said good luck."

"I will. Be sure to rest that leg."

"Okay, doctor."

No smile in sight. He turned away and headed downstairs to do whatever Fran had hired him for.

Cinnamon decided to stay out of his way. She'd prop her leg up, ice it, and spend the afternoon closeted in the suite, searching for jobs and sending out queries and second emails to the colleagues who hadn't responded to her original message. Maybe make a few cold calls too. Plenty to keep her busy.

She wouldn't venture downstairs again until he left for the day.

BY MIDAFTERNOON NICK had washed all the windows from the inside except those in Cinnamon's suite. Ditto for collecting paint chips. The suite would have to wait—it was almost time to pick up Abby and Sharon. Trouble was, he needed the chips now, as first thing Monday morning he intended to stop at the hardware store and get the paint custom-matched.

At least, that's what he told himself as he stood outside Cinnamon's door, as uncomfortable as a kid about to meet with the school principal. He lifted his fist to knock but faltered. He hadn't seen her since he'd helped her to the Orca Suite after the visit with Doc.

On the drive home she'd made him nervous with her questions. He'd cut her off fast, and managed to be civil enough. So had she, but they'd both been ill at ease. He felt weird about the whole thing and didn't want to leave for the weekend until he made things right. Plus, he needed those chips.

He rapped on the door. "Hey, are you okay in there?"

"Yes, thanks."

He shifted his weight. "I need a couple of paint chips to match at the hardware store. Do you mind if I open the door and come in?"

"No."

She was nestled in the oversized armchair that faced the cloudy view, her laptop open on her lap and her legs propped on the matching ottoman. Except for her slipper socks they were still bare. Rosy lamplight lit the room, and a cheery gas fire blazed in the fireplace.

A cozy image, except for the bandage on her shin and the pained expression on her face. A result of the injury, or his being here? He stood in the threshold, leaning his

ANN ROTH

shoulder against the doorjamb. "How's the leg?"

"Bearable, as long as I keep it propped up."

"Do you need a refill on that icepack?"

"Not yet."

"You're smart to work stretched out like that."

"At the moment I don't feel very smart."

"Anyone could've slipped on those wet steps. When I come back Monday, I'll lay nonskid tape on each riser. That should help, and ease Fran's mind. She nearly had a heart attack when I told her what happened to you."

"I spoke with her too—twice before I was able to convince her that I'm going to live." A brief smile flickered and died. "The nonskid tape sounds like a good idea."

She cast a worried glance at the laptop, and he guessed the crack about not feeling smart was more about that than the accident. "How goes the job search?"

"Not so well."

"With your background there must be dozens of companies interested in you."

"You'd think. I contacted my consultant friends about that, but they don't seem to want to…" She cut herself off, sighed, and dropped her gaze. "I though sure at least one or them might know of a job opening or have an idea where to look, but I haven't gotten much

104

help."

"Bummer."

"Yeah." Frowning, she fussed with the hem of her sweater, smoothing it down. A moment later her chin jutted up. "No worries—I've been looking at various consulting companies online. Something's bound to come up."

"I'm sure of that."

An uneasy silence fell between them. Now was a good time to make things right. Nick pushed away from the doorjamb and wandered into the room, scrubbing the back of his neck. "On the drive here this morning, you seemed put out with me."

"You started it. I was trying to make conversation. I don't even know how I offended you."

Her prickly tone didn't make this easy. "You didn't."

But asking about the magazine article she assumed he'd read had cut too close for comfort. No one knew how difficult reading was for him. Shame burned like acid in his gut.

"Is that why you told me to 'leave it' and drowned me out with super loud music? If you don't want to build your business, then say so."

Nick hung his thumbs from his belt loops. "I'm comfortable, and the work is mostly steady. Hell, I own my own house. That ought to tell you something."

All right, a three-room cabin and a small, detached workshop, but it was paid for. Though he needed a bundle of cash for Abby's math camp, and Sharon could use some financial help… None of that was Cinnamon's concern. Nick narrowed his eyes and crossed his arms. "Why are you so interested my life?"

"I'm not," she said, slapping the laptop shut. "You brought up this morning and I'm finishing the conversation."

"You're too damn nosy for me. I'm not one of your clients, and I don't need your help." His temper was climbing. With effort he reined it in. Cinnamon's mouth opened, but he cut her off. "You weren't exactly friendly either, not before and after you got those stitches."

"I was trying to be independent."

"Yeah, I got that. Why did you let me think you were fired from your job, when you quit?"

Her turn to tense up. "Resigned," she corrected. Her expression remained calm, but her back went soldier straight. "What exactly did Fran tell you?"

"Nothing. That's why I'm asking. Isn't it better to quit than get fired?"

Her hands started their fidgety routine, rubbing circles over the closed laptop. "That depends."

"On what?" he asked, genuinely wanting to know.

"The problem was... personal."

"What'd you do, tell the boss to shove it?"

She laughed without humor. "Not exactly. I... It's not a story I want to share. It's private."

"And my business isn't?"

"Touché." She settled into her chair again, looking far more relaxed. "We're quite a pair, aren't we??

"You can say that again." Relieved that the tension between them had eased, he turned to leave.

"Nick? Don't forget to wish Abby good luck from me."

This was the second time she'd offered good wishes and the first time he smiled. "Will do."

It was only on the drive home that he realized he'd forgotten to get a paint chips from her suite. He shook his head, wondering at his forgetfulness and not pleased that Cinnamon affected him so strongly.

In so many ways they were wrong for each other. He knew that in his head, yet when he was near her, reason and logic seemed to fade.

Good thing he was headed out of town for a few days—he needed to get his mind off her. Busy with Abby, he wouldn't think about her all weekend.

Surely by Monday, she'd be out of his system.

Chapter Ten

NICK SHEPHERDED SHARON'S car down the two-lane road that would eventually lead to the freeway and Portland. Though it was nearly five o'clock and rush hour, traffic was light. In the off season in rural Oregon, it generally was.

Her old sedan didn't have the pep of his truck, but it had a back seat. After a long, hard week, Nick's sister had readily agreed that he should drive the four hours to Portland and that Abby should sit up front. Now, her head cushioned by a pillow, Sharon slept soundly in the back. In the passenger seat up front, his niece was as quiet and still as her mother, but not asleep. Nervous, Nick guessed, but in the early darkness of winter he couldn't quite make out her expression.

"How're you doing?" he asked in a low voice so as not to disturb Sharon.

Abby gave him a withering look and answered with a question. "Why didn't you and Mom say something?"

"About what?"

"You know what—that the cranberry factory might close. You should've told me!"

And here he'd thought her solemn air had been due to tomorrow's math bee. Praying Sharon was awake now, because he sure as hell didn't want to deal with the scary subject alone, Nick shot a hopeful glance in the rearview mirror. Still out cold. He was on his own.

"Where'd you hear that?" he asked, buying time while he figured out what to say.

"Everybody at school's talking about it."

"At this point, it's only a rumor," he assured her. Which was mostly true.

"I still have the right to know."

"You've been working so hard to prep for the math bee. We didn't want you to lose your focus. Face it, kid, you're a worrier."

"That's a lame reason! I'm not a baby anymore, so quit treating me like one!"

Her dramatic tone was almost comical, but her hurt feelings and the possible factory closure were nothing to joke about. "Do you think we don't know you're growing up? I swear we'd have told you if there was anything to tell."

By her crossed arms and angry huff, she wasn't buying that.

"There's a town meeting about the situation next Tuesday night, and—"

"What's going on up there?" Sharon said from the back.

"We're talking about the factory." Nick gave her a help-me look at the rearview mirror.

"You hid your problems from me. I'm coming with you to that town meeting," Abby insisted. "That way, I'll know the same stuff as you."

Sometimes his niece was too damn smart for her own good. "Brother," Nick muttered.

"Now that she knows, she should come," Sharon said. "Don't you think, Nick?"

Why not? Abby was dead-on—she had the right to know. He shrugged in agreement.

Satisfied, the girl uncrossed her arms.

A sign pointed to the upcoming freeway entrance. Nick glanced at her again. "You hungry, kid? 'Cause once we get on the freeway it's another two hours to Portland. This is a good time to stop for dinner, get gas, and stretch your legs."

"I'm not eating tonight," she announced.

She was at the age when she was always hungry, and this surprised him. "What?"

"Well, I am," Sharon said. "I'm starved."

Abby glanced over her shoulder at her mother. "We should have brought sandwiches to save money."

So that was the deal. He sighed. "This is exactly why we didn't tell you about the factory."

Sharon nodded. "Stewing over what hasn't even happened yet won't do any good, and certainly won't help you win the math bee."

"Your brain needs nourishment, both tonight and in the morning," Nick added, because that kind of logic usually worked on Abby.

"I'm not sure I want to win anymore," she mumbled in a voice so low he figured he'd misunderstood.

He frowned. "Say what?"

"If Mom loses her job, how will we pay for my room and board at math camp?"

Sharon didn't offer any answers, and Nick knew she was fretting about the same thing. Not that she could pay those costs even if she kept her job. The bulk of that expense weighed on his shoulders.

"You leave that to us, okay? We'll get you there," he assured her.

Maybe Cinnamon was on to something—he needed to boost his business, and fast. He thought about asking her for advice, but his pride wouldn't let him. Besides, she might expect him to read that article, a chore that could take decades. He'd always managed on his own, and would find his own way forward. And he wasn't going to think about her this weekend.

Yet he couldn't help wondering where her job search might land her. Why in the world had she resigned from what had to be a high-salary position without a new job lined up?

Not his business, and he had enough problems without worrying about her. But here he was, doing it anyway, wishing he could hold her and ease her troubles in a very physical way.

As his body stirred to life, Abby released a heavy sigh.

"Okay, I'll eat, but only if we go somewhere cheap."

"You got it, kid." Crisis averted.

"I see a fast-food place on the left ahead." Sharon pointed out the window. "And a gas station on the same side of the street."

"How lucky can you get?" Slowing, Nick signaled and pushed Cinnamon from his thoughts.

AT THE DINER Friday, Andie set a throw pillow on a café chair and waited as Cinnamon carefully propped up her leg. "How does that feel?"

"Pretty good," Cinnamon replied, touched by the restaurant owner's attention and concern.

"If it still hurts, I could bring you a glass of whiskey…." Andie's eyes widened comically.

Cinnamon laughed and shook her head. "If this was dinner instead of lunch, I'd take you up on that."

The woman nodded. "I'll be back with unspiked coffee." She flashed a smile. "Sorry, Cinnamon, you had your chance."

The gentle teasing made her feel liked, a welcome change from the hellish months since Dwight had gone back to his wife. Thanks to her sore shin she hadn't slept well, and a yawn slipped out.

"You're tired. Are you sure you're up to meeting the Friday girls?" Fran's gaze touched the five empty chairs around the table, soon to be filled with the women she lunched with every other Friday in the off-season. "I hope so, as everyone wants to meet you."

"I can't wait to meet them either. I've heard about them forever. Besides, you made a special trip back to the Oceanside to pick me up for this." Cinnamon glanced at her shin. "Since you won't let me drive."

"It won't hurt you to rely on other people for transportation for a day or two."

"Yeah, but after lunch, you're stuck driving me back

again."

"I'm happy to do it. I wish I could spend the whole afternoon with you. But with the Valentine's Day dance in two weeks and the Love on Main Street outdoor art show coinciding…" Fran shook her head. "I'm heading up the entertainment committee, and I'm stuck."

"Hey, I'm a big girl. I don't need you to babysit me."

Although without Fran, the Oceanside seemed way too quiet. Too bad Nick was in Portland…

Cinnamon frowned. Hadn't she already wasted enough time fixated on the man? During brief snatches of sleep last night she'd even dreamed about him. Vivid, erotic scenarios filled with all sorts of fun and deliciously naughty things. Her woman parts tingled and ached.

"Your face is all red," Fran said.

Not about to comment on that, Cinnamon changed the subject. "What exactly is the Love on Main Street outdoor art show, and isn't this a risky time of year to display art outside?"

"We do it at the Fall Festival in October too, and draw quite a few people. We put up a giant, open-sided tent in the town hall parking lot, with heaters inside. The carvings, sculptures, drawings, and paintings are done by locals and must depict love in some way—of the sea, the beach, Dunlin Shores, lovers, pets, anything. We have a great time. Too bad you'll be gone by then."

Not only gone, but hopefully about to start a new job. Cinnamon crossed her fingers. And yet… "I'm sorry I'll miss that."

"Some other time. Did you have better luck with this morning's job search?"

Cinnamon shook her head. "I called a few of the colleagues who didn't reply to my earlier email. No one picked up. I left messages, but I don't expect to hear back. I'm sure that by now, the word is out that I was forced to resign. Which doesn't exactly make me a prize catch."

For a moment anger and disappointment darkened her world, but she refused to let negative feelings get the best of her. "Their loss," she said, raising her chin.

"Absolutely." Fran's eyes flashed indignation. "If you ask me, your colleagues are a bunch of lame-brains. Discounting your considerable skills and experience simply because your relationship with the boss went sour is ridiculous. Especially after you've proved yourself over and over again."

"We're on the same page there. Still, looking back, I wished I'd used better judgment."

"Hey, we all make mistakes. Anyway, you don't get a do-over. Cut yourself some slack."

Cinnamon wasn't sure she could. "Don't worry about me. I'll find my way. I always have." As long as she got a job before her savings ran out. She trembled at the thought.

"Tough, feisty, and determined—that's the Cinnamon I know and love."

"That's me, all right."

"On top of your job worries, you go and get hurt. I feel terrible about that."

"It's not your fault I fell."

"You slipped on my wet steps, making what happened very much my responsibility. If you sue me, I'll understand."

Cinnamon's jaw dropped. "I'd never do that. I'm better today than yesterday, and in a day or two I'll be good as new. Be glad it was me who fell, and not someone else."

"I'd rather no one get hurt. I'm glad Nick can fix the problem. He promised to pick up some of that nonstick tape first thing Monday morning and put a strip on every step—provided the weather cooperates." Fran glanced out the large picture window fronting the street, where a sleeting rain much like yesterday's pummeled the glass. "For safety's sake, let's hope for a sunny Monday."

There she went, mentioning Nick, and just when

Cinnamon had managed to get him out of her brain.

Steaming coffeepot in hand, Andie hastened over and filled two mugs. "Speaking of Nick," she said, picking up the conversation as if she'd been at the table all along, "any word on how Abby did at that math bee this morning?"

Fran shook her head. "I thought sure Sharon would text, but she hasn't. I doubt we'll hear until they get back, which could be late tonight."

"If you hear anything, let me know."

"I will, and you do the same. I need to run to the ladies' room before everyone arrives," Fran said as the waitress bustled off. "Be right back."

Cinnamon nodded, and wondered if the bubbly girl had won the math competition. Sharon's silence could mean bad news. Cinnamon hoped not.

Her thoughts turned to Nick. Why did she continue to dream about him when she wanted a man who valued the things she did. The opposite of the attractive handyman who gave her heart palpitations. Face it, she was in lust, big-time, and no amount of self-talk could fix that.

If only he hadn't come to her room yesterday afternoon, with his wary expression and that sexy tool belt hanging low on his narrow hips. After the accident and the brush-off by her colleagues, she'd been upset and vulnerable, and hadn't wanted to engage with anyone. Especially Nick.

But his willingness to talk about the tension in his truck had made her want to trust him. She'd actually considered talking about Dwight. But she was too ashamed. Anyway, he hadn't exactly been forthright with her either.

"I'm back." Fran slid into her seat. "I wonder where—" Suddenly the door opened and a group of women trouped in. "There they are." She smiled and waved.

Five hands waved in return. The women hung their coats on the coat tree. Then, chattering as if they hadn't seen each other in years, they made their way to the table. One by one they introduced themselves to Cinnamon, each expressing sympathy over her injury.

Betsy—at thirty, the same age as Cinnamon and Fran—was married with grade-schoolers and owned a yarn shop. Lynn, divorced and the town's postmistress, and Claire, who owned and ran the dry cleaner's, were about ten years older. Joelle and Noelle, never-married fraternal twins and retired bed-and-breakfast owners, were well past seventy.

Talking and laughing and smelling of damp, fresh

air, they arranged themselves around the table, Betsy beside Cinnamon, and Joelle and Noelle directly across from her.

They seemed as colorful and as much fun as Fran had said. Her spirits brightening, Cinnamon looked forward to a lively lunch.

Chapter Eleven

"I HEAR YOU like to shop," Betsy commented as the Friday girls lunch get-together wound down. "But who doesn't, right?"

Cinnamon liked the woman, who was relaxed and easy to talk to. "I wish I could shop, but while I'm unemployed I'll stick to browsing."

"That's fun too. I had a real slow morning at the yarn store, so I closed for the day. The kids don't get home from school for another two hours, and I'm free until then. Why don't I show you some of our shops." She glanced at Cinnamon's leg. "If you feel up to it. Either way, I'll drive you back to Fran's."

Refusing to give in to her injury, Cinnamon smiled. "Sounds fun. I'd love to see your store. There must be a lot of knitters around here."

"You'd be surprised," Betsy said. "Tourists buy yarn too."

"Would you mind if we stop at the Cranberries-to-

Go shop? I met Liz, the owner, at the doctor's office yesterday and said I would."

Her new friend's eyes widened. "I'll bet she didn't appreciate seeing Nick with you. Was she nasty?"

"The opposite—she was friendly. I think she sensed there's nothing between Nick and me."

Every woman at the table appeared to be listening, and Cinnamon spoke to them all. "We're hardly even friends."

"He drove you to Doc's," Betsy pointed out.

"So? I'm sure he'd have done that for anyone."

"Maybe, maybe not," replied Lynn, the postmistress sitting on Betsy's other side. An intent expression brightened her weathered face as she leaned around Betsy to catch Cinnamon's eye. "See, Liz has a thing for Nick, and everyone knows it. One time when they ran into each other at the post office, Liz did everything possible to seduce him." Lynn pantomimed sticking her finger down her throat. "Pushing her breasts out, running her hands down her hips, and licking her lips... Ugh. It's a good thing no kids were around. He ignored her, bless his heart."

"It's not just Nick," Fran said. "It's any available male."

Lynn gave a knowing nod. "She's way too needy. It

scares men off."

Andie, at the table to refill mugs, shook her head. "I feel sorry for her. She's been through some rough times. She got pregnant and married while she was still in high school. The marriage didn't last. Her ex moved away without a forwarding address, leaving her when Bret was just a baby."

Joelle and Noelle, the aging twins, added their opinions.

"A real tough situation," Joelle sympathized. "But you gotta hand it to her because she did—"

"—get her GED." Noelle nodded. "And worked her way from a clerk—"

"—to owner of Cranberries-to-Go," Joelle finished.

"That's admirable," Cinnamon said. "Nick says she's looking for a man to settle down with."

"That can't be true." Lynn looked surprised. "She's been divorced nearly twenty years and loves to flirt. Wonder where he got that idea?"

"Maybe she proposed," Joelle said.

The entire table laughed.

Cinnamon shrugged. "All I know is what he told me. Anyway, Liz's son is nineteen, only thirteen years younger than Nick," she added, quoting his very words. "She's too old for him."

Inwardly she frowned. Here she was, thinking and talking about Nick. Again.

Joelle and Noelle offered matching sage nods. "Liz isn't the only woman who's tried to catch him," Joelle said. "But he's never dated the same woman for long. I—"

"—wonder why that is?" Noelle posited.

"What do you think, Cinnamon?" the twins asked in unison.

The question drew the interest of everyone at the table including Andie, who was stacking dirty plates onto a tray.

"I wouldn't know."

"My guess is, he hasn't met the right person," Fran said.

Talking about Nick made Cinnamon uncomfortable, especially with six women scrutinizing her. "Shouldn't you be getting to your meeting?" she asked Fran. "Betsy will drive me home."

Fran glanced at her watch. "I almost forgot! Thanks, Betsy." Grabbing her purse, she jumped up, setting off a chain reaction.

"You're a lovely young woman." Joelle smiled at Cinnamon. "We must do this again—"

"—before you leave town." Noelle patted her blue-gray perm. "We usually meet every other week, but for you we can squeeze in an extra lunch. How about next Friday?"

"WE'RE HERE." BETSY pointed at the red and white Cranberries-to-Go sign hanging over the door.

Cinnamon had spent the last hour browsing the shops with her new friend, with a sit-down break to rest her leg in between. They got along well, and she was nearly as comfortable around Betsy as she was with Fran.

Funny, she'd never felt this relaxed around her colleagues. But then, she'd been so wrapped up in work that she'd never thought to develop a true friendship with a coworker. Any socializing had been done at business functions and over an occasional drink after work, nothing more.

How pathetic was that? No wonder coworkers had snubbed her after Dwight broke things off.

She peered through the window, glimpsing aprons and other items decorated with cranberries. "I see some cute things in there."

"Cute enough to go inside?" Betsy asked.

"I told Liz I'd stop by. What's the big deal?"

"She's been after Nick all these years, and he was with you at Doc's."

Cinnamon groaned. "We went over this at lunch, remember? Nick has never been interested in her, and she knows it. Besides, there's nothing between Nick and me. He's not my type." Moving as fast as her injury allowed, she opened the door and limped through it.

"All right, but don't say I didn't warn you," Betsy murmured, following her.

Except for them, the small store was empty. Liz brightened. "Hello there. You're my first customers in ages. I was about to close up shop."

Betsy nodded. "I had the same problem today. I locked up before noon."

Liz glanced from Cinnamon to Betsy. "You two know each other?"

"We met today at lunch."

"Ah, the Friday girls thing."

Apparently everyone in town knew about the get-togethers. Of course they did. Dunlin Shores was a small town.

"I can't buy anything today," Cinnamon said. "But I wanted to see your shop."

"That's okay. How's your leg? Does it still hurt?"

"I think I'll live, thanks."

Liz arched one brow Betsy's way. "How's that darling husband of yours?" She smiled at Cinnamon. "Cal's my

CPA, and I adore him."

"You adore every man," Betsy muttered.

If Liz heard, she didn't let on. "Any news on Abby, Cinnamon?"

"Not that I've heard."

"I thought for sure Nick would have called or texted you by now."

Betsy snickered under her breath, as in I told you so. Cinnamon frowned. "Why would he do that?"

"I saw how he looked at you in Doc's office, and I figured…" Crafty smile. "You know."

What was this, a conspiracy? "You figured wrong," Cinnamon corrected for what seemed the dozenth time. "Nick brought me to Doc's because he had to. We're not involved, and he doesn't have feelings for me."

"Think what you want, but I've known him for years. He's never looked at me that way." Liz leaned toward Betsy. "Like he wanted to eat her for lunch. If he just once looked at me like that, I'd be head-over-heels and halfway to heaven."

Cinnamon knew that look first-hand. Even thinking about it made her feel tingly and hot. "Even if I wanted to get involved with Nick, which I don't, there's no time. In less than two weeks I fly back to L.A."

For what, she didn't know. Not a job… yet.

"That's enough time for a fling," Liz said.

Betsy nodded. "She's right."

Cinnamon gaped at the woman she'd spent the past few hours with, wondering whether she knew her at all. She hadn't told her about Dwight, but they'd discussed relationships and men in general. "I'm not the fling type," she said.

Liz smiled. "Maybe you should be."

Betsy's cell phone rang. "Excuse me," she said, slipping it from her shoulder bag and walking away as she answered.

"I'm going to look around now." Turning away from Liz and more talk about Nick, Cinnamon wandered off, past shelves of foods, knickknacks, and personal care products that contained cranberries or the juice. She picked up a porcelain plate decorated with cranberries and noted the full set of matching pieces, all the while musing over Liz's suggestion.

Have a fling with Nick?

She certainly lusted after him enough. But affairs were something her mother did, without a thought for the future. Cinnamon was different, reserving sex for serious relationships. She'd had her share of those, and thanks to bad luck, not one had lasted. She didn't have affairs.

Although if she were honest, the relationship with Dwight qualified.

True, at first she'd assumed that after his divorce, they'd get married. But after months of sneaking around, she'd known it wouldn't happen. Yet fool that she'd been, she'd hung on. In the end, what they'd shared was a sleazy affair that had cost her the job she loved and ruined her career.

Nick didn't want to get serious with anyone, and right now neither did she. What was wrong with giving into temptation? If no one got hurt…

Shocked at herself, Cinnamon pulled a cranberry cookbook from a display and mindlessly leafed through it. She was *not* going there with Nick, and why had Liz put the idea in her head?

Never mind. In ten days she'd leave. Till then, she'd close off her emotions, just as she had at Sabin and Howe.

Compared to the months she'd spent stifling her feelings there, ten days was nothing.

Chapter Twelve

MONDAY DAWNED CLEAR and crisp—great weather to fix Fran's slippery steps. Rested and pleased at Abby's success, nonskid tape and tools in hand, Nick whistled as he strode across the deck. He avoided thoughts of Cinnamon. Out of sight, out of mind had worked well, and whether or not he saw her today, he intended to keep his mind on his work.

With a long list of chores, that shouldn't be hard. He headed through the slider in search of coffee and nearly plowed into Cinnamon. Coat on, keys in hand, she appeared to be on her way out.

"You're in a big hurry," he said, looking her over. Her eyes were bright and her skin glowed with good health. She was more beautiful than ever.

Her cheeks flushed and her gaze darted away and he realized he'd spoken out loud. His turn to go hot-faced. Yet he couldn't look away. It'd only been a few days, but he couldn't believe how good it was to see her. Or how much he wanted her.

So much for getting her out of his system.

He set down his tools and supplies. "Where are you off to?"

"I'm meeting Betsy for coffee."

She didn't seem interested in making conversation, which should have been a relief. It wasn't.

Nick scratched the back of his neck. After they'd talked Friday, he'd assumed they'd cleared the air. Wrong. Better off with her being distant. Maybe he should leave things alone. "If you're going out and wearing long pants, your leg must be better," he said instead.

"Much."

"That's good news."

"I hear you have good news too. Abby took first in the state math bee for her age category—wow! You and Sharon must be so proud."

"We are." He grinned and puffed up his chest. "She's bouncing all over the place."

"I can picture that. Congratulate her for me?"

"Sure thing."

Silence.

Not quite ready to let her go, Nick kept talking. "I'll be doing paint touch-ups today. I still need samples from the Orca Suite to match at the hardware store. Okay if I get them this morning?"

"If you can do it while I'm gone, that'd be great."

She didn't quite meet his eye, instead stared at his shoulder and fiddled with her keys, their jingling the only sound in the room. Every clink upped the tension between them.

"I'm trying like hell to make conversation, and you can't wait to get out the door," he said. "Are you running late or still upset about Thursday? Or did I do something else to make you mad?"

Abruptly the jangling stopped. "It's not you."

He waited for her to explain, but she didn't. So he pushed. "What is it, then?"

Still no direct eye contact. "Please, don't ask."

"Got it." Not his business, but he wanted to know. Seriously irritated for caring, he pivoted toward the kitchen, picked up the mug Fran had left by the coffeemaker, and filled it. Knowing he'd be working inside today, he'd left the thermos at home. "Where's Fran?"

"Picking up a gift for Abby, something from both of us."

That last part surprised him so much he nearly snorted his coffee. "You only met her once."

"And I like her. I admire her too. She's amazing." At last she met his eyes.

Nick didn't understand the sudden change in her mood, but his spirits lifted. "You should've seen her, Cinnamon. So calm and cool. With all the stress of competing, I never figured she'd be able to relax. Watching her up there was amazing." He shook his head in wonder. "Where she got those smarts, I don't know. Not from our side of the family."

"You're no dummy, Nick."

She wouldn't say that if she knew how bad he was at reading. For a moment, he dropped his gaze to the dark liquid in his mug. "Anyway, you'd have enjoyed watching her."

"I wish I'd been there. Did she use your breathing technique?"

"Yep. Anytime you want me to teach it to you, I'm here." His offer surprised him, but then, he was talking out of desire.

Where had he come up with the cockeyed idea that all he needed was a few days away to forget about wanting her? One friendly glance and he was gone.

"I'll think about it."

Her lips parted a fraction, the bottom lip full and tempting. Drawn by a force he couldn't fight and hardly aware of what he was doing, he set down his mug and moved toward her.

Cinnamon swallowed. "What prize did she win?"

Her expression posed a different question that had nothing to do with Abby and everything to do with Nick.

She wanted him.

Which was more arousing than any fantasy. He was so focused on her and so hot for her, he wasn't sure he could form the words to speak. Somehow he managed. "Two weeks at an elite math camp this summer, tuition paid."

He'd saved enough for the required deposit on her room and board. The rest he'd earn even if it meant working twenty-four-seven.

"She must be so happy." The hot gleam in Cinnamon's eyes burned into his soul.

God, he wanted to kiss her. He stuffed his hands into his jeans pockets. "It'll give her a good start toward getting into college."

"Yes," she breathed, as if she'd heard his thoughts.

She was impossible to resist. He cupped her chin. Her skin was smooth and soft and warm, and beneath his palm her pulse jumped wildly. "You mean that?"

"I don't know what you're talking about."

"Sure you do. I have this big problem—I'm attracted to you, but I don't want to be."

"I understand completely. That's why I was cool a little while ago—trying to keep my distance." She gave her head a slow shake. "We're not right for each other."

"Yet here we are." Stroking her jawline with his thumbs, he coaxed her face up. Her eyelids lowered, the thick lashes dark against her skin. "You have no idea how much I want to kiss you right now."

"I think I do." She pulled in a shuddering breath. "What should we do about that?"

"The only thing we can do—get this over with so we can put it behind us and move on."

The keys dropped from her fingers. "You think that'll work?"

"Whether it does or not, I'm going to kiss you."

Forget stopping Nick before it was too late. Cinnamon needed his kiss the way she needed air. Every nerve and muscle in her body primed and aching, she met him halfway. It seemed like forever before his mouth covered hers, tentative and soft, a teasing brush of flesh against flesh.

She didn't want teasing. She wanted passion. Now.

"That's no kiss," she said against his mouth. Impatient and suddenly ravenous, she threaded her fingers through his dark hair as she'd longed to for days, and pulled him closer. Somehow her coat had come off, bringing them into more intimate contact. Standing on her toes, her sore shin forgotten, she planted a fevered kiss on his lips.

"Very nice," he said, "but not enough."

His arms wrapped around her and anchored her tight against his hard body. "Open your mouth."

She did. He slanted his head and slipped his tongue inside. She tasted coffee and hunger. Lost herself in a haze of sensation—the taut strength of Nick's arms, the solid warmth of his body, the scent of pine soap and man. Her heart pounding, she breathed his breath and shared hers in turn.

Already damp between her legs, she hooked her calf around his thigh and cinched herself closer. Like her, he was aroused.

A growl rumbled in his chest. He slid his hand to her aching breast. One touch and she was ready to combust. With very little effort she'd climax.

The force of her need scared her. Nick was wrong for her. All wrong.

"Nick." She unhooked her leg and pulled back. "We

can't do this."

His breathing ragged, he released her. He glanced at the bulge straining against his zipper and offered a humorless smile. "Looks as if our experiment failed."

Cinnamon swallowed. No amount of logic could erase her longing for release, both for herself and Nick. She couldn't do this, wouldn't.

To keep from reaching out to him, she scooped up her coat and keys. "Betsy's waiting. I have to go now."

She pivoted away and hurried through the sliding door.

Chapter Thirteen

FEELING SNEAKY IN a good way, Fran accompanied the mayor and the other three town council members into the small conference room inside the town hall building. In a bold-faced lie she'd told Cinnamon she was at another Valentine's Day planning committee meeting. She closed the door behind her and joined the others at the oval table.

Mayor Eric Jannings, owner of Jannings Real Estate, Anne Trueblood and her law partner, Pete Sperry, and Chet Avery, principal of Dunlin Shores High School, four professionals who worked at demanding, full-time jobs but found the time and dedication to set the town budget and create the policies that helped Dunlin Shores run smoothly. All eyes were on Fran.

"Thanks for meeting on such short notice," she said. "I know you're wondering why I called this emergency conference when I'm not even on the council, so let me get right to the point. The cranberry factory is about to go under. We have to do something about that."

"Which is why we're holding a town hall meeting tonight." Mayor Jannings fiddled with his pen and eyed her with raised eyebrows. "Why the secrecy, and what's so important it couldn't wait?"

"I think I know a way to save our factory, an idea I wanted to share before tonight." She had their full attention. "You all know my friend Cinnamon Smith is visiting from L.A."

Chet nodded. "Abby mentioned that. She says Miss Smith is real nice."

"That's true," Fran said. "FYI, she prefers to be called by her first name. She's a top-notch consultant and between jobs at the moment, though probably not for long. Her expertise happens to be helping companies on the verge of bankruptcy. She's saved dozens, some in worse shape than the cranberry factory. The other day she toured the place and talked with some of the people who work there, and she's aware of the problems." She paused, then delivered the idea that had broadsided her a few hours earlier. "I think we ought to recruit her to save it."

During the thoughtful silence that followed, the mayor stroked his chin, Chet tapped a pen against his lips, and, Pete and Anne scribbled on their legal pads.

"She probably charges an arm and a leg," Anne said at last.

"I was thinking the same thing," the mayor said. "We don't have the money."

Which Fran knew from a conversation with Cinnamon some days ago. "That's where you come in. As the mayor you have clout, and Tate might listen to you. Why not call him and convince him to hire her?"

The mayor stroked his chin again. "It's worth a try, but Tate's a tough nut. Anyway, he's pretty much thrown up his hands on the whole thing."

"Hello—you could sell a cranberry bog to a person looking for vacation property."

Pete nodded. "Don't ask the man, sell him."

Mayor Jannings straightened his shoulders, the movement causing his blue sports coat to strain across his bulky shoulders. "All right, I will."

"Could you do it right away?" Fran asked. "Cinnamon will be at tonight's meeting. If we could start off with the good news that Tate is going to hired her, people will leave feeling hopeful." Including Cinnamon, who'd seemed unusually glum and edgy last night and this morning, no doubt over worry about the lack of job prospects.

For the first time, Anne smiled. "Heaven knows, we

could all use a dose of optimism."

"It's a good plan," Chet chimed in. "But even great salespeople fail sometimes. What if Eric doesn't convince Tate to hire her?"

"Then we'd better have plan B ready," the mayor said. "Suggestions, anyone?"

Anne fiddled with her pen. "Isn't that why we called tonight's meeting? To gather ideas on how to save the factory?"

"We're bound to get a few worth pursuing. Still, we should each come with ideas of our own."

Fran shared hers. "Even if Tate doesn't want to hire Cinnamon, we should ask her for advice."

"Let's hope she has some."

"LOOK AT THE size of this group," Cinnamon commented as she and Fran entered the town hall behind a throng of worried locals. "Are you sure it's okay for me to take up a seat?"

Fran gave her a don't-be-silly look. "Of course. I want you to see how our town works and meet the mayor and city council members," she said over the buzz of conversation vibrating through the spacious room. "And on the selfish side, this is a way to spend time with you."

"You had me at 'of course.' " Only six days left before Cinnamon headed back to L.A. for… She still had no idea. No job offers had come through, which was unsettling, to say the least. The familiar fear knotted her stomach, but she didn't want to think about that tonight. She forced a smile. "I'm so glad you suggested I come visit."

Fran looked guilty. "I know I've said this before, but I'm truly sorry I haven't spent more time with you."

"And I've told you a dozen times, I'm fine by myself. Anyway, for the last eight days we've seen each other more than we did in the past five years."

Two men and a woman dressed in business suits waved and started forward. Fran waved back. "Those three are on the town council. Come on, I'll introduce you."

Cinnamon pushed through the sea of people, pleased that she recognized several familiar faces. Even strangers greeted her with smiles. She exchanged hellos with Dr. Bartlett and Lynn from the Friday girls. On the side of the room, she glimpsed Liz chatting with two somber-faced male companions.

"Look at Liz," she commented to Fran. "A teenage boy on one arm and a man on the other. Neither one looks happy about that."

"Bret is her son, and Drake is her brother."

Cinnamon's jaw dropped, and Fran chuckled at her obvious surprise before she sobered. "Both work at the cranberry factory, and you can understand why they're worried. Look, there are Joelle and Noelle." Cinnamon and Fran both smiled.

They ran into Andie and two more Friday girls, including Betsy. Cinnamon met her husband and adorable young son and daughter.

So many friends. She almost felt as if she belonged here. She gave her head a mental shake. No small-town living for her. She loved the energy that pulsed through big cities and the variety of restaurants and entertainment options available. But amenities and hustle-bustle couldn't compensate for the warmth of the people in Dunlin Shores.

Why was she even thinking about this? There were no job opportunities and few if any available men with the qualifications she wanted.

All right, she wanted Nick—on a physical level only. She glanced around, searching for him and his family, but didn't see them.

Could he kiss… With his skilled mouth alone, he'd ignited her hunger in ways she still didn't understand.

He'd certainly blown her plan to wall off her emotions straight to hell.

He was probably a fantastic lover too. The thought set her body humming, the familiar ache blooming in all her private places. She'd never know. As badly as she lusted after him, she couldn't handle a quick fling.

Thrown by her feelings she'd stayed away from the Oceanside for the rest of the day, first spending time with Betsy, who to her relief hadn't mentioned Nick at all, then driving aimlessly through the winding hills surrounding Dunlin Shores. The dark sky and endless rain had suited her mood. Later she'd parked herself at the library. Using her phone, she'd searched out information on various consulting firms.

She'd returned to the Oceanside after five, when Nick was sure to be gone. Today he'd stayed away, claiming work elsewhere. A huge relief, as avoiding him seemed the safe thing to do.

Yet even as she reminded herself, she craned her neck and continued to search for him. Catching herself, she frowned. If she were smart she'd change her plans and leave tomorrow.

"Here they come," Fran said, indicating the council members. "Let's save seats for ourselves." Gesturing at two folding chairs, front row, center, she slipped off her jacket. "Give me your coat."

As she tossed both wraps on the seats, the council members reached them. She made the introductions. "Cinnamon, meet Anne Trueblood and Pete Sperry, law partners, and our high school principal, Chet Avery."

The council members shook her hand and welcomed her. "You must be so proud of Abby Mahoney," she said to Chet.

His face lit up. "She's a talented student."

"The entire town is thrilled," Anne said. "Has Fran mentioned our plans to salute Abby at next week's Valentine's Day dance? I hope you'll be there."

Cinnamon thought again about the warm, open people she'd met, all of them welcoming her with open arms. She bit her lip. "Unfortunately, I'll be gone by then."

"She leaves for L.A. next Monday," Fran explained. "Unless…"

Cinnamon didn't miss the sly glances her friend and the council members exchanged. "Unless what?" she asked.

Instead of answering, Anne smoothed the jacket of her navy wool suit and asked her own question. "Have you enjoyed your visit here?"

"More than I ever imagined. Dunlin Shores is beautiful, and the people are friendly." Especially Nick, who put a whole new spin on the word.

Pete beamed as if she'd complimented his family. "We'd like to increase our tourism business, so spread that around, will you?"

"Here comes Mayor Jannings." Anne nodded at the portly, balding man striding toward them, his progress hampered by the people who greeted him. "He'll want to meet you."

Cinnamon had no time to wonder why before the introductions took place.

"Any friend of Fran's is a friend of mine," the mayor said. "I'm only sorry my wife isn't here. She'll be along soon, and I know she'll be delighted to meet you."

It was almost as if they were wooing her. What for? Cinnamon eyed Fran and received an innocent smile.

"Well," Chet said, "we'd best head to the stage. Nice meeting you, Cinnamon, and again, welcome to Dunlin Shores."

The mayor and the other city council members made their way up the wooden steps to the podium onstage.

A tingle climbed Cinnamon's spine and she sensed someone staring at her. Even before she glanced over her shoulder, she knew who it was.

Nick.

A forest-green flannel shirt draped his broad shoulders and abs in an oh, so sexy way. As his gaze locked on hers, everything else faded. She moved toward him.

Chapter Fourteen

NICK HADN'T EXPECTED to see Cinnamon tonight, but there she was. Beautiful, desirable, and headed in his direction.

"Look—there are Fran and Cinnamon!" Abby raced toward them, somehow avoiding crashing into anyone.

Sharon followed. Nick hung back, fighting a losing battle to keep his distance as Cinnamon's welcoming gaze tethered him to her like an invisible string.

He'd given up fighting his hunger for her. What was the point, when he thought about her all the time?

Still, he didn't budge until Abby drew her attention away. Trudging forward, his hands curled into fists at his sides, he focused on his niece. Anything to distract his mind and help him keep his hands off the woman whose kisses and softness still burned in him.

Abby beamed at Cinnamon and Fran. "Thanks so much for the bookstore gift certificate! Mom's taking me there on Saturday."

"You're both so sweet," Sharon gushed, still aglow over her child's success despite the grave circumstances of the evening's town meeting. "Abby loves to read, and so do I."

"Me too," Cinnamon said. "Books have always been a huge part of my life. I couldn't live without them."

Nick didn't read unless forced. More the reason to keep his distance from her. As Cinnamon, Fran, and his family discussed favorite books and authors, he hovered behind his sister, shifting around and hoping nobody asked him for his favorites.

"You read a lot, and you're top in the state in math!" Fran grinned. "I feel as if I know a real celebrity."

Abby covered her mouth with her hand and giggled.

"Hey, can we sit with you?" Sharon asked, gesturing toward the empty seats in the front row.

Nick understood why those spaces were vacant. Most people hated to sit in the front, himself included. He would've preferred sitting in the back. With his sister and niece heading for the empty seats, he had no choice but to follow.

Sharon and Fran flanked Abby, leaving two chairs for Nick and Cinnamon.

"You and Cinnamon get to sit together," Abby said with a wide grin.

Stuck beside her—pure torture. Wasn't tonight bad enough without this? Careful not to touch her—that would be dangerous—he sat down. "I didn't expect to see you here."

"Fran invited me, and I want to know what happens." She caught her sweet lower lip between her teeth, then lowered her voice. "About yesterday…"

He knew its softness and the taste of her mouth, wanted to taste her again. "What about yesterday?" To his own ears, he sounded gruff.

"I—"

Whatever she was about to say was cut off by the loud squeak of a microphone. Standing at the podium, Mayor Jannings fiddled with the thing and tested it again. When all was well, he nodded at the crowd and offered a polite smile.

"Good evening and thanks for coming on a work night. What a great turnout, but that's one reason why I love this town. I know you love it too. The council members and I called this special meeting because we're in crisis. The cranberry factory is on the brink of closing. It's my hope that together we'll figure out what we can do to save it, and tonight I encourage you to share your ideas."

Nick noted Sharon's frown and Abby's grave expression. From his seat he couldn't reach either of them. Wanting to offer his sister a reassuring shoulder squeeze, he stretched his arm behind Cinnamon. Sharon gave him a weak smile.

He caught a whiff of Cinnamon's floral scent. All by itself, his hand brushed her back and lingered a moment. She sucked in a breath that sounded like desire, then stiffened. Nick removed his hand, but the damage was done. His body went on red alert, and the semi-erection that had plagued him all day threatened to go full tilt. Like he was fifteen years younger and inexperienced.

Mad at himself for thinking about sex when his sister's job was at stake, he sat up straight and leaned forward, staring hard at the podium and straining to concentrate on Mayor Jannings.

That worked a little, but he knew where he stood. In lust hell, with no way out.

CINNAMON TRIED TO listen to Mayor Jannings, but with Nick beside her, awareness of anyone else was difficult. Especially now that he'd slipped his arm around her. Only to reach his sister, but the way he touched her back had set off a longing inside. She wanted to nestle into his warmth, silently promising him more later.

But that wasn't going to happen. Locking her hands around her purse strap, she shifted away from him.

Mayor Jannings had asked for ideas. A grizzled man she recognized from the factory stood, and the mayor nodded at him. "Yes, Charlie?"

"If we started earning a profit again, we'd do all right, wouldn't we?"

"How're we going to do that, when our machinery is so darned old it breaks down constantly?" a man called out from the back. "We can't compete like this."

"You said it, Vince!" a woman shouted.

Angry people throughout the room yelled out thunderous agreement.

The mayor held up his hands for silence. "We can't discuss the problem if everyone talks at once," he stated loudly into the microphone. "One at a time, please. You'll all get your chance."

Hands shot into the air.

"Claude Jenkins, you have the floor."

The thin, graying man who stood appeared to be close to retirement age. "I've been with this factory forty-odd years and I've seen things go from good to okay to bad. I agree with Charlie, but I also agree with Vince. Given our situation, how're we going to make a profit?"

The man named Vince jumped to his feet. He was

JUST THE WAY YOU ARE

about Nick's age, with a stocky frame, wearing a Dunlin Shores, Oregon, sweatshirt. "Even if Tate won't give us new machines, he could sink more money into advertising. That'd help."

"He hasn't bothered to do that over the past eight years. Why should he start now?" asked a middle-aged woman with frizzy hair. "He's got a string of successful businesses. He doesn't need us. If we don't figure out a way to make money, we're history."

A woman moaned, and grumbles again filled the room.

Still standing, Vince crossed his arms. "We don't even have a general manager anymore, just Drake, Claude, and me trying to run the place without knowing what we're doing. Today the mixer jammed a good ten times. It's so old, nobody remembers how to do much except unclog it and pray. We had to close down one whole processing unit. Only the good Lord knows when we'll be able to use it again."

"Uncle Nick can fix that machine so it won't ever break again," Abby's girlish voice rang out. "Maybe he'll invent a whole machine like he did with the sorter my mom uses."

Nick, an inventor? Did he own the patent, and why hadn't he mentioned this talent? Cinnamon squinted at him.

"That's a great idea!" Sharon grinned at her brother.

Shouts of "Nick! Nick! Nick!" pounded through the room.

To Cinnamon's surprise his face flushed red and he ducked his head, as if he couldn't handle the attention. She'd never thought of him as shy. He certainly wasn't around Fran or her, and he hadn't been at Andie's the other night. This was different.

"Stand up," Sharon urged him.

"I think they want you to say something," Cinnamon added.

"No way. Lay off."

His forbidding frown included both of them, before his attention centered on his lap. Over his bent head Sharon shook her head.

Liz's brother rose. "Drake Jessup here. You don't have to stand up or say anything, Nick. Just stop over to the factory tomorrow and give us a hand. We'll pay you out of the supplies fund, but don't tell Tate."

Nervous laughter erupted through the room, providing a needed respite from the tension and worry.

Nick eyed Fran. She expected him to return to work at the B and B in the morning. "The Oceanside can wait," she said. "You go ahead and do what you can to help the factory."

He nodded. "I'll be over first thing tomorrow," he said loud enough for everyone to hear.

"Thanks," Drake called out.

A young woman with cocoa-colored skin stood. "I'm Becky Johnson and I run the sorter with Sharon. Even if Nick fixes the problem, we'll be lucky to make up what we lost today, never mind turning a profit. You must know something we don't, Mayor Jannings. Are they gonna shut us down, and if so, when?"

"That's a fair question, Becky. I spoke with Randall Tate this afternoon and asked him that. I also suggested he hire a consultant to help turn the business around. I recommended someone who happens to be sitting in the front row in this very room." He looked straight at Cinnamon. "Cinnamon Smith, a close friend of Fran Bishop's, is an expert at saving companies on the verge of bankruptcy. She's good at it too—I checked."

Stunned, Cinnamon gaped at the man on stage while wild applause broke out.

"Wahoo," Fran crowed, shooting her a big grin.

Abby shrieked, and Sharon clapped louder than anyone else.

Cinnamon looked at Nick. He shrugged. "I had nothing to do with this, I swear."

"I haven't finished," the mayor said in a booming voice. He looked and sounded so solemn, the crowd immediately quieted. "Due to cost considerations, Mr. Tate declined to hire Ms. Smith or any other consultant. He repeated what most of us already know—if he can't sell the factory over the next few months, he'll shut it down."

Heavy silence greeted the statement, and Cinnamon could feel worry in the room. She felt awful for the people she'd come to know and like, especially Sharon, Abby, and Nick. What would they do?

"Any nibbles from potential buyers?" a man asked from the back.

The grim-faced mayor shook his head. "Not as of this afternoon."

The tension mounted. A tall woman in rimless glasses stood. "We're in a catch-22. No one wants to buy us because we're not profitable, but we won't be profitable until someone sinks some money into the business."

"I have an idea," Cinnamon said in a voice only Fran, Sharon, and Nick could hear. "What if—"

"Tell everyone," Fran urged.

Sharon nodded. and Nick gestured for her to stand. Cinnamon raised her hand.

"Our expert consultant has something to say," the

mayor said.

She rose and pivoted to face the group. "What if all of you buy the factory?"

Stunned expressions greeted the question. "Interesting idea," the mayor said. "How would we go about doing that?"

"And how can we afford it, when most of us are struggling to make ends meet?" someone asked.

"You may not need much cash. There are attorneys who specialize in employee buyouts. They'd have to figure all that out." She glanced at Pete and Anne, seated on-stage. "Do either of you know of someone?"

The attorneys conferred quietly. "We might," Pete said. "I'll check first thing tomorrow and report back."

The mayor nodded. "I'd appreciate that."

"Tate brought in his own general manager, but he quit," Drake said. "Our last local G.M. was Willis Tilden, and he's in the cemetery. There's nobody else around here to run the place."

The town council members exchanged blank looks. Meanwhile, from the floor, individuals fired off questions.

"How would our buying the place guarantee a profit?"

"What do we know about running a business?"

"How're we going to get money to upgrade our equipment?"

"What if we lose our shirts?"

From the back of the room, a rail-thin male who looked about sixteen stood. "My name's Eddie Wilkins," he said in a surprisingly powerful voice that boomed through the room. "I like your idea, Miss Smith. If you're Fran's friend, I trust you. Will you help us?"

Cinnamon considered the offer, which was exactly the kind of project she enjoyed. Earlier tonight, hadn't she wished she could stay here longer? This was her chance to do that. But she needed a job that paid decently. Working with factory employees who didn't have much to spare for a business teetering on bankruptcy, she'd be lucky to earn anything. How would she pay her bills and rebuild her savings? As much as she wanted to help, she couldn't. She opened her mouth to explain, but Fran cut her off.

"Cinnamon's services don't come cheap. She commands high fees and deserves every penny. How would we pay her?"

Cinnamon could have hugged her for stating her concerns.

"She needs to earn her living, just as we do," another understanding soul somewhere in the back called out.

The energy level in the room plummeted. Shoulders slumped and people stared at the floor.

"You can have all the money in my savings account," Abby said as she scrambled to her feet. "Ninety-six dollars and fifty-three cents."

Heartfelt murmurs all around. Touched, Cinnamon smiled at the girl. "You're a sweetheart, Abby, but—"

"If the factory closes, my mom and lots of her friends will lose their jobs," the girl interrupted, the words tumbling over each other as if she were afraid slower speech might be easily stopped. "We'd have to move away, to a place where we don't know anyone." She looked as if she were about to cry. "I don't want to leave Dunlin Shores and my friends, and I don't want to be the math bee champion for some other school. Most especially, I don't want to move away from Uncle Nick. He already told my mom and me he's not moving. Won't you please help us?"

The entire room went dead silent, everyone awaiting Cinnamon's answer. The plea deeply moved her. Her heart broke for the girl, her family, and the friendly town. But as much as she wanted to help, she couldn't survive without a decent pay-check.

She bit her lip. "I can't take your money, Abby."

Beside her, Nick cleared his throat. "Take mine,

then. That machine I'm about to fix? Give my pay to Cinnamon."

Stunned, she turned toward him. Before she could thank him and refuse, other offers peppered her.

"From now on you'll stay free at the Oceanside," Fran said.

"Eat anytime at Andie's, on the house," the diner owner called out.

"That shin I patched up?" Doc shook his head. "No charge."

"I'll give you free knitting lessons and all the complimentary yarn you need," Betsy promised.

"And free goodies from Cranberries-to-Go," Liz said.

Offers of free groceries, movie rentals, and gas followed.

Although the generosity of these people, who didn't have much to begin with, was mind-blowing, Cinnamon's knee-jerk response was to turn them down. Throughout her childhood she and her mother had lived hand-to-mouth, often relying on handouts. This wasn't the same, yet somehow it felt that way. She wanted and needed money.

"Well?" Nick's soft words were for her ears only.

He didn't touch her, but stood so close she felt the warmth from his body. She wanted to look at him but didn't dare. She couldn't bear to see the disappointment on his face when she refused the job and let the people of Dunlin Shores down.

She opened her mouth to refuse the offer. "All right, I'll help you," she said instead.

Shocked silent by her own words, she sat down hard, to cheers and energetic conversation that shook the rafters.

"I need money—I can't take this job," she stated, her words lost in the noise.

Apparently Nick heard her. His smile was warm and grateful. "I think you just did." He lifted her hand and kissed the back of it. "Thank you."

The warmth of his lips almost made up for the fear in her heart.

Chapter Fifteen

Between clanking machinery, employees calling out to each other as they worked, and oldies tunes belting from someone's radio, Nick couldn't hear himself think. Lucky for him, installing the new rotator wasn't difficult. The hard part had been yesterday, when he'd mulled over what to do as he studied the defective mixer and taken the engine apart. He'd brought the rotator home and had spent the rest of the day and half the night designing and fashioning what he needed out of the odds and ends stashed in his workshop. That and installing the new rotator this afternoon had taken two full days.

He sure hoped the thing ran. Then he could finish the work at Fran's, move on to the other jobs that paid, and get on with saving for Abby's camp room and board. Cinnamon said she didn't want his pay from this job, but he planned to give it to her anyway. He didn't begrudge her the money. His first priority was doing what he could to help the factory survive.

The camp people had their deposit and didn't want the rest until mid-July, a good five months from now. Plenty of time to save up—as long as Sharon didn't lose her job.

Nick slipped his screwdriver into his tool belt. He swiped his hands on his jeans and nodded to Cliff Baxter, the mix operator. With his long neck and bobbing head, he reminded Nick of a chicken.

Standing at the control panel, Cliff waited until Nick joined him before pushing the start button. The engine purred to life, its huge metal blade rotating exactly as it should.

"She's good as new," Cliff hollered to his coworkers. "Thanks, buddy." He clapped Nick's shoulder.

"No problem." His work here was finished. Employees around the area whistled and waved. The attention made him ill at ease, and he gave a terse nod. Eager to leave, he swung toward the door on the other side of the factory.

And froze. Cinnamon was walking toward him with the confident, sophisticated grace people expected of a woman with her smarts and background.

Dressed in expensive pants and a matching sweater that hinted at her curves, she looked elegant and every inch the professional consultant. Totally out of place among the jeans, lab coats many workers were required to wear, and hair nets.

While he, an uneducated handyman, fit right in with his faded jeans and old work shirt.

Not counting occasional glimpses of her moving around the factory interviewing workers and taking notes, he hadn't seen her since the town hall meeting two nights ago. But he thought about her nearly every waking moment, and had enjoyed a few erotic dreams too. He wasn't the only man who drank in the sight of her. Several other guys on the floor looked too. He scowled at the room in general, warning them off.

"Hi, Nick."

Oh, that smile. It lit him up inside, and he returned it. Then reminded himself that she was here more or less under forceful persuasion. Word was, she'd agreed to stick around two more weeks, then leave for good. Back to life in the big city.

He sobered. "How's it going?"

"I could use a few more hours' sleep at night, but other than that, not bad."

"I haven't been sleeping much, either," he admitted, glancing at the mouth that drove him to distraction.

She flushed, and her eyes softened, the same as after those kisses he couldn't seem to forget. The lust that had plagued him since she'd first arrived at Fran's ignited.

He jerked his gaze to her shoulder—as if that helped. "Are you sorry you took this job?"

She shook her head, surprising him. "Actually, I'm enjoying myself."

She noted the look on his face, and laughed. "I'm shocked about that too. I've been working late, researching the cranberry industry, and I've learned some interesting facts. Did you know that over the past decade, the world-wide demand for cranberry juice and frozen cranberries has dropped?"

"No, I didn't. We sure drink enough of the stuff around here."

"Apparently this town is the exception to the rule. In order to survive we need to look at manufacturing other cranberry products. Your sister and some of the other employees are meeting right now to brainstorm ideas."

Nick was impressed. "I don't think anybody ever asked them to do that."

"If they had, the factory wouldn't be in the mess it is now. Employees are the experts. They'll come up with better ideas than I ever could."

"Cool. What happens then?"

"A team researches the best product ideas, then the accountant and marketing people look at the financial considerations and what the factory can afford. Then test the products on the market, evaluate a few months later, and tweak where needed."

She oozed enthusiasm when she talked about the plans. He chuckled.

"What's so funny?" she asked.

"You're all fired up. I like that."

"This is what I love to do."

"No wonder you're good at it. Have you considered going into business for yourself?"

"I've never even been tempted. I need regular, steady paychecks. I wouldn't get that with self-employment."

"What are you scared of? With your attitude and brain it's a safe bet you'll have more work than you can handle."

"I'm not a big risk-taker."

The conversation ended. Silence hovered between them, broken by the whir and clang of machinery. Ready to leave, Nick turned toward the exit. "I'll be going—"

"I found an attorney—"

They both spoke at the same time.

"What did you say?" Cinnamon asked.

"You first."

"I found a lawyer to help with the employee buyout. He'll be here on Monday. Vince and Drake offered to sit in and represent the rest of the employees."

Nick nodded. "Sounds as if things are moving along."

"I'm pleased. You should be too, for doing your part."

"You mean fixing the mixer? Piece of cake." He made a flip gesture with his hand. "Anyone could do it."

"That's not true. You have a gift, Nick, and you shouldn't dismiss it. I know people who'd kill to have your talent."

High praise that made him feel good, but also un-comfortable. He shoved his hands into his pockets. "Whatever," he said and clamped his mouth shut.

"Okay." She seemed puzzled by this. "You wanted to say something earlier?"

"Yeah—I'm finished here and leaving."

"Do you think we could talk first?"

Now what? "Go ahead."

"It's too noisy out here. The general manager's office is much quieter."

On the way, wary, he squinted at her. "What's this about?"

"Come in and I'll tell you."

He followed her inside.

NOT ENTIRELY SURE what she was doing and wondering at herself for jumping into who knew what, Cinnamon preceded Nick into the office. He'd totally confused her. She'd meant what she'd said, that he was skilled at designing and building machines, and had intended to start a conversation about what that could mean for his future. But he'd brushed off her words.

Out of modesty, or a total lack of interest? A week ago she'd have guessed the latter. But now, having seen his uneasiness at attention and praise at the town hall meeting and again a few minutes ago, she had her doubts.

He deserved recognition, money, and more, and she was determined that he get it. Although what she was about to suggest could make him as tense and silent as he'd been when she'd mentioned building his business on the drive home from Dr. Bartlett's.

She was about to find out. A little nervous, she closed the door to the office. Instant silence. "Now we don't have to shout."

"What's this about?" Nick repeated.

He seemed as on edge as she was. Stalling, she gestured at the coffeemaker on the adjacent counter. "Do you want coffee? I'm caffeined out, but there's plenty left."

"I'll pass. I've tasted the stuff they call coffee around here. It's nasty." His mouth quirking—much better than the frown he'd given her moments ago—he sank onto the lone visitor's seat across the desk, a sagging plaid-covered thing that looked as uncomfortable as her wobbly, wooden desk chair.

The tension in the room faded, and as she took her seat behind the scarred metal desk she laughed at his expression of disgust. "That's something we completely agree on. Tomorrow I'm following your example and bringing a thermos of Fran's coffee with me."

"Smart woman."

When he smiled at her, he was so attractive. Face it, even wearing a scowl he was gorgeous.

He knew it too. His suddenly hot eyes traveled from her mouth to her breasts. Her nipples hardened. She forgot she wanted to talk to him about his work and the talent he played down, forgot that she was determined to do everything possible to get him the recognition and money he'd earned for his efforts at the factory.

She wanted to slip around the desk, sit on his lap and kiss him until they were both breathless and ready for more... A sigh of longing slipped out.

"This is why you invited me in here? To proposition me?"

"I would never do that!" Not intentionally. Self-conscious and embarrassed, she straightened the papers on her desk. "This is about factory business. The sorter you designed is impressive—simple yet ingenious. How did you get the idea?"

She'd expected his modest shrug. "The one Sharon operated kept breaking down, and I invented something better. To make her job easier."

"And you did." About to tread on delicate matters, Cinnamon posed a question she already knew the answer to. "I assume you were paid decently for your work?"

"I didn't do it for the money, I did it to help my sister. Tate never even knew."

"That's not fair to you." Lacing her fingers together atop the desk, she leaned forward. "Tell me you've at least applied for a patent.

"Why would I do that?"

"You designed a piece of equipment that, from what my research shows, is far more efficient than any other sorter in use. You deserve to get paid for that."

He snorted. "Right. The factory can't even pay you."

"It makes some of its money thanks to you, and you should be compensated. Once the employees take over and the company begins to turn a profit, you deserve a percentage of that. The same goes for any factory in the country or the world, for that matter, that uses the machine you invented. You can earn royalties, Nick, potentially a good deal of money."

He leaned his forearms on the desk, his face reflecting confusion and disbelief. "I don't see how."

"The way it works is, if you hold the patent and this or any other business chooses to use your design, they pay you for the privilege. Otherwise they're stealing your genius and profiting from it, while you get nothing."

"I'm no genius," he said, all gruff, "but I do want that money. How do I collect?"

Relieved and happy that he was interested, Cinnamon went into consultant mode. "First, you file for a patent." She handed him the papers she'd prepared earlier. "I downloaded the forms and printed two copies of everything. All you have to do is read through the documents and fill them out."

She didn't understand his pained expression. "You can do that on your own, but if I were you, I'd get legal counsel before sending anything to the U.S. Patent Office. I contacted Pete and Anne, and they suggested an attorney who—"

"You what?"

He didn't raise his voice, but his warning tone was impossible to ignore. Cinnamon swallowed, but it was too late to stop now. Besides, she saw nothing wrong with what she'd said or done, and refused to be intimidated. "I asked Pete and Anne for the name of a good patent attorney around here. The closest person they know lives about sixty miles away. That's a long drive, I know, but at least you don't have to go all the way to Portland." She slid a slip of paper across the desk. "Here's her number."

Nick ignored it. "Did I ask you to do that?"

"No, but I thought—"

"You didn't think at all." The small tic she recognized pulsed in his jaw. "If I wanted your help I'd ask for it. I don't." He collected the papers and phone number stood. "Stay out of my business."

He left the office, shutting the door none too gently behind him.

Chapter Sixteen

"THEN HE WALKED out," Cinnamon told Fran that evening over dinner. Tonight Fran had made chicken and dumplings, and they ate in the dining room at home. "I seem to have a knack for making him mad."

Recalling the harsh set of his shoulders when he'd walked out, Cinnamon winced. At least he'd taken the papers. Mission accomplished, right? And she felt awful.

Her appetite ruined, she pushed her plate aside. "I wish I knew why he was so mad."

"Nick's a very private person. If the situations were reversed and he was poking into your life, how would you feel?"

A few days ago, he'd posed a similar question. Should've paid more attention. "When you put it that way…" She gave a sheepish shrug. "I was only trying to help. Nick deserves money and recognition for his invention. He won't go after those things without a push."

"True," Fran mused. "But I think it's more than that. You care about him."

"Only as a friend."

"You don't expect me to believe that. I am your BFF, and I can read you like a magazine."

Cinnamon was starting to care for Nick as more than a friend. "You're right," she admitted. And that scared her even more than not having a job lined up.

ALONE IN HIS kitchen, Nick hunched over the patent registration papers he'd been working on all evening. Yawning, he massaged his aching neck and checked the time on his cell phone. Close to midnight. No wonder his neck had a crick in it.

He frowned at the papers spread out on the table. Four hours spent deciphering what looked like hieroglyphics to plow through a whopping two pages of instructions, reading and rereading until it made sense. He'd managed to fill out most of one page. Only a few million to go.

You're not stupid, you just see words differently than most people. That's what Mr. Edison had said back in high school. Maybe, but Nick felt pretty damn thick-headed. And fed up.

At this rate he might finish by Christmas. If he was lucky. Unfortunately, December was ten months away and he didn't have that kind of time.

Sharon could help. As soon as the thought entered his mind he shut it down. His sister barely had enough time for her own bills and paperwork without taking on his. Then there was nosy Abby, sure to wonder why he wasn't doing the work himself, or worse, tell someone her uncle couldn't take care of his own business.

Nick squirmed at the thought. He'd rather swallow battery acid than have his niece or anyone else know he found reading so hard. Especially Cinnamon.

In his mind he pictured her, warm and admiring as she praised his sorter invention and the mixer repair. That had felt good. Still did. He smiled. If she found out he couldn't read she'd never look at him like that again. Likely she'd never look at him at all.

Damn her for poking her nose where she had no business sticking it and shackling him with work he had no time for. In a fit of frustration he swore, crumpled the nearly completed page into a ball and lobbed it into the trash can.

And instantly regretted it.

What about the money? Cinnamon said he stood to

earn a bunch. If she said so, he believed her.

He sure as hell needed money, for Abby's camp and her college tuition. He wouldn't mind paying off Sharon's debts and making her life easier.

Not gonna happen without that patent.

The paper with the patent lawyer's phone number was within reach. May as well ask the expert for help. Cinnamon had suggested it, even said she'd do the same.

Asking a lawyer to do his paperwork would cost plenty. He'd bring the woman the completed forms instead, then get her advice.

Nothing to do but buckle down and finish the sucker. He retrieved the crumpled paper and smoothed it out. Rubbing his tired eyes, he bent again to his work.

Chapter Seventeen

L<small>ATE</small> M<small>ONDAY</small> <small>AFTERNOON</small>, fresh from a trip to the patent lawyer's and ridiculously pleased with himself, Nick headed straight for Cinnamon's office. The door was closed. He was in such good spirits he didn't let that stop him. He knocked, then peeked in.

Sitting at the battered, old desk that should have been tossed on the scrap heap, she looked up from her laptop.

"Hey," he said. "You busy?"

She gave him a sideways look. "That depends. Are you going to bawl me out again?"

Nothing could dampen his high spirits. "Not unless you poked your nose into more of my business." He tempered the words with a half-smile.

"I think I learned my lesson." She shut the laptop. "I shouldn't have pushed you, Nick, and I'm sorry."

"That's what matters," he teased. "Can I come in?"

She nodded, and he strode inside, closing the door

behind him. Whistling softly, he sauntered over and sat in the wobbly chair, and cut straight to the point. "I came to apologize too. I was out of line. I know you were trying to help."

"Of course I was. I'm glad you realized that. You're in a good mood today."

"I am. I just got back from the patent lawyer you recommended. She checked the application and said everything looked fine. She'll do a search to make sure no one else holds a patent on my invention. Then she'll send it to the patent office."

Cinnamon beamed. "Now, that's good news."

"Yeah." He grinned like a fool. "I told her about some of my other inventions and she said she'd research those too."

"There are others?"

Her astonishment tickled him. "Six more," he said, puffing out his chest. He stood. "That's what I came to tell you. I'll let you get back to work."

She rose and came around the desk. "Nick Mahoney, you're an amazing and talented man."

This time he accepted her high praise and returned it. "You're not so bad yourself."

"Look at us, all full of mutual admiration." She extended her hand. "Congratulations."

She wanted to shake hands? He wanted more. Any other day he would've fought the hunger simmering inside, but he was flush with his success. "Hey." He threaded his fingers with hers. "I'm not some casual business associate."

"I know." Desire flared in her eyes.

He tugged her hand and drew her closer. Her lips parted, an invitation tough to resist. As badly as he wanted her, moving forward could be dangerous. There was too much heat between them, and once they started, no guarantee he could stop—and no way to keep him from getting trampled when she discovered he wasn't the man she thought he was. Because sooner or later she would.

"Nick?" She slid her palms up his chest. "What's happening between us?"

He'd never noticed the tiny gold flecks in her eyes. As he delved into those rust-colored orbs, they seemed to shimmer and beckon him closer. Lust swirled through him, fogging his brain. "This thing between us isn't going away. It's growing stronger—too strong to resist."

With his free hand he cupped her chin. She caught her breath, licked her lips. And just like that he was rock hard.

"What are we going to do about it?" she asked.

He started to kiss her, then hesitated. "Here in the office?"

"Good point." She pulled away to lock the door, then returned to him. "I believe you were about to kiss me."

AS KISSES WENT, this one was sizzling. In seconds flat Nick went from turned on to crazed. Hard and throbbing, he gripped her sweet ass and anchored her as close as possible. And loved her mouth, her tongue with his.

"I want to touch you." He cupped her breast.

"Wait." Breathing as if she'd sprinted through the factory, she pulled away. "My silk blouse will wrinkle in the wrong places, and everyone will know what we did."

"Easy fix—get rid of it."

Nodding, she unbuttoned the blouse slowly—too slow for him. With fingers that trembled, he nudged her hand aside. "I'll do that."

When he finished the job, she took the blouse off and draped it over the back of her desk chair. The lace on her bra covered her nipples. He traced them with his thumbs and felt them stiffen.

Cinnamon moaned. "Can we sit down? My legs are about to give out."

He glanced around the room. Wobbly chairs, metal desk, stained carpet. He refused to stoop that low. "Let's try the counter—"

"How about the counter—" she suggested at the same time.

With a low laugh he grabbed her hand and pulled her toward it.

Cinnamon pushed the coffeemaker aside, and he lifted her up. "Where were we?"

"Here, I think." She placed his hands on her breasts.

He touched and caressed, then lowered his head and tasted her through the bra. She made little sounds of pleasure that drove him wild. He wanted to do so much more… His turn to pull away. "Why don't you get rid of that bra."

It disappeared. Her breasts were small but perfect, with proud, pink nipples. "I've been imagining what your breasts looked like since that day you fell and hurt your shin."

"That's a long time. Are they what you imagined?" she asked, thrusting her chest out.

Nick groaned. "They're beautiful, and you're making me hot. Now I can taste you the way I want to." He licked and suckled and teased until she writhed and wrapped her thighs around his hips.

He took her mouth, holding back nothing. She kissed him the same way. He shifted closer—as close as two fully clothed people could get. It wasn't enough.

She clutched his shoulders and tensed. He wanted to make her come, wanted deep inside her, his need so powerful it totally freaked him out.

What the hell was he doing? This wasn't supposed to happen.

Straightening, he untangled her legs from his hips. "We need to stop."

She looked dazed. Her hair was wildly messy, and her face, neck, and breasts were flushed—as if they'd had sex.

God above, he wanted that.

He scooped her bra off the floor, then brought her the blouse. "It's not wrinkled at all."

"Good." She quickly put them on, then slid from the counter.

They'd started down a path he should've steered clear of, but it was too late now. They wanted each other, and he refused to apologize for something he didn't regret. "I never figured we'd get this carried away. Things got awful hot, awful fast."

She didn't look sorry either. "We're both to blame."

"I'll see you later." He started toward the door. His hand on the lock, he paused. "You'll want to comb your hair and fix your makeup."

Her hand flew to her hair. "Don't you dare unlock that door until I do."

"Brother," he muttered, but she had a point. He glanced at his erection—it was taking awhile to go away—and figured he ought to wait a moment too. Despite his condition he felt good.

Within a short time, she looked pretty much as she had when he'd first come into the office. Except for the flushed skin.

All business now, as if that could erase what they'd shared, she smoothed her clothes, then waved at the door, which he unlocked.

"Thanks for stopping by, Nick, and once again, congratulations on filing the patent," she said as he opened it.

With a nod, he left.

Chapter Eighteen

STANDING AT THE sorter, Becky Johnson elbowed Sharon. "Look who just came out of Cinnamon's office."

Sharon pushed the stop button to see. "What's Nick doing here? He didn't mention coming in today." For once, he looked happy. She adjusted the hairnet she was required to wear for sanitary reasons. "He fixed the mixer and designed us a better sorter. He has lots of jobs waiting, so why is he here, and what was he doing in her office?"

"By that smile he's wearing, it must be something good. Maybe Cinnamon offered him a job."

As if. Sharon snorted. "My brother would never work here. Why would he, when he likes being his own boss? At least he and Cinnamon are getting along. They didn't start off that way."

"Getting along? Are you blind, girl? Have you seen the way he checks her out when she isn't looking? Or that hungry look on her face when he walks into the room? They ought to get together. Maybe they have."

"I wouldn't bet on it," Sharon said. "They're total opposites. Besides, Nick doesn't get close to anyone."

"Well, it's pretty darn clear he wants to get close to Cinnamon. If he hasn't made a move, he's missing out."

Sharon doubted he'd made any move on Cinnamon, but it was an interesting thought…

Her friend settled her hands on her ample hips. "I know that gleam in your eyes. You're cooking up a plan to help him along."

"It's true, he needs a push, but if I stick my nose into his private business, he'll kill me."

"You're going to do it anyway. What have you got in mind?"

"Nothing yet, but Fran knows them both. I think I'll give her a call."

RAIN SPATTERED THE windows of the Orca Suite, and the wind howled. But the cheerful fire that warmed the small sitting room blunted the bad weather. Staying in seemed a good idea today, which was why Cinnamon had opted to revise the factory projections remotely.

A brisk knock sounded at the door. "It's Fran."

Cinnamon smiled. "Come on in."

"I'm about to leave for the town hall to finalize the decorations for Saturday's Valentine's Day dance, and I'll be gone awhile."

"Don't worry about me. When you get back, I'll probably still be here, working. But if I go out, I'll text you."

"You're not going to the factory? You didn't mention that at breakfast."

"I didn't decide until I thought about going out in this mess. Don't worry, I checked in with Drake and Claude. They don't care where I work."

"They'd better not. For the past week you've spent ten hours a day at Tate's, including last weekend. You deserve to stay right here in front of the fire. I made a fresh pot of coffee—you mentioned taking a thermos with you from now on."

"Don't worry, it won't go to waste. I'm sure I'll drink at least a thermos' worth. I'll see you when I see you."

"Great, but FYI, some of that coffee is for Nick. He'll be here soon to fix your ceiling fan."

The mere thought of him in the suite sent Cinnamon's body into a frenzy. The two days since she'd last seen him had left her aching for him. His mouth, his hands… She could so end up in bed with him.

But sex without love?

She needed to think more about that. She hadn't mentioned anything about her and Nick to Fran, couldn't when she had no idea what she was doing or where it would end.

"Thanks for letting me know to expect him" she said, doing her best to seem nonchalant. "I think I'll take a break."

"Tell me you're not going running today. Your shin just healed, and even with the nonskid strips on the steps you could slip."

That accident had started all the trouble with Nick. Not true. From the moment he'd taken her bags from the trunk of the car she'd had a thing for him.

Cinnamon shook her head. "I learned my lesson about running in a downpour. I'm going to get a mug of coffee, browse the bookcase downstairs, find a good novel, and lose myself in it. Something to keep me out of Nick's way when he shows up."

"You have feelings for him."

"Is it that obvious?" Cinnamon groaned. "Promise you won't say anything."

"You know me better than that."

"Don't look so darned pleased either. Nick and I will never get together."

"He's a terrific guy. And now, with more than one invention soon to be patented, he'll meet your requirements for a man with money in the bank. With his skills and smarts, a boatload of money."

Cinnamon didn't doubt that. Nick wasn't the white-collar executive she pictured in her life. He was an inventor—so cool—and creative people didn't have to dress certain ways or work regular hours.

Why was she thinking like this? The intense feelings between her and Nick were physical, nothing more. Anyway, she was leaving town a week from tomorrow.

Irritated with herself and Fran, she scoffed. "You missed your calling. You should be in the matchmaking business."

All innocence, her friend widened her eyes. "I'm only stating the facts. Don't forget about the Valentine's Day dance Saturday night. Nick will be there, and with love in the air that night, who knows what will happen?"

"Will you stop? I'm not sure I'm going to the dance, but I do plan to visit the Love on Main Street art show. I might even buy something."

Dipping deeper into her dwindling savings would hurt, but Cinnamon couldn't imagine leaving Dunlin Shores without some memento. At the moment she couldn't imagine leaving, period. But she had to go where the job took her—once she landed a position.

She wasn't as worried about that as she had been. A few days ago a Boston-based company she'd queried online had contacted her to set up a phone call with one of the partners. After a fairly lengthy conversation, he'd set up another interview with the other partner via Skype. That too had gone well.

"You'll love the art show. You can't miss the dance either. It's a huge event. Everyone in town goes, and that includes tourists. I've been working really hard organizing and chairing the decorations and entertainment committees, and I'd like you to see the end results. Plus, you're my bestie, and I really want you there." She looked sideways at Cinnamon. "Oh, and we're making a big fuss over Abby that night. You can't miss that."

Cinnamon laughed. "All right, I'm sold—for Abby, and because it sounds really great. I don't want to hear anything else about Nick."

"Fair enough. You know, you could stay longer. Unless that consulting firm in Boston hires you."

"I expect a job offer soon." Which was awesome, or so she tried to convince herself. She'd grown so attached to Dunlin Shores, the possibility of a job on the opposite side of the country didn't feel as exciting as it should.

"I'm happy for you, but depressed for me," Fran said.

"I wish you could stay."

"There aren't any job opportunities here. We have another full week together, which is longer than we thought."

"And the whole town is grateful." Fran cocked her head. "I think I heard Nick come in." She moved to the door. "I'll see you late this afternoon."

Cinnamon managed to check her hair before he appeared in her doorway.

Dressed in jeans and a flannel shirt, tool belt on his hips, he carried a stepladder under his arm. Raindrops glistened in his windblown hair, and his face was ruddy from the cold and wind. It all added up to one gorgeous male.

Her breasts tingled, and she crossed her legs to stifle the ache between them. "Good morning," she said, sounding breathless to her own ears.

"You're not supposed to be here." He set the ladder down and looked her over, his gaze traveling down her body as if he knew exactly where she most craved his touch.

"Yes," she murmured, wondering what she'd agreed to.

"Okay." His lips quirked.

"Um, yes, go ahead and fix the fan." She jumped up, grabbed her laptop, and hugged it.

Chapter Nineteen

"YOU'RE HUGGING THAT laptop awful tight," Nick commented as he set the ladder down.

Like a shield, Cinnamon realized. As if it could protect her from herself. "I was going to head downstairs and read while you do your thing with the fan." And pull herself together.

"You read on your laptop?"

"Not unless it's something for work."

"Why don't you put it down."

She set it back on the desk.

Nate unbuckled his tool belt, the casual act somehow so intimate she blushed clear to her toes. "What are we doing?" she asked as he laid it on the carpet.

"How else am I supposed to give you a proper hello?" He stepped in close, tipped up her chin, and kissed her. Deep, warm, filled with promise."

She had no idea how long the kiss lasted, but by the time he let her go, she forgotten everything but him.

"That's better. Looking at that fan—" he pointed upward "—I see that I don't need my tools to take it down. My hands will do the job."

He flexed his fingers, big and callused, but oh, so skilled at turning her on…

Cinnamon caught her breath. "If you're trying to seduce me…"

"Trust me, I've thought about it."

Fighting the urge to invite him into her bed right now, she bit her lip. Although there was no reason to hesitate. The instant his lips had claimed hers, she'd made up her mind—she wanted sex with him. "So that's going to happen?"

"Depends."

"On what?"

"What you want from me. I'm not looking for anything serious."

"Me either." Short-term and no strings. If she was careful to keep her heart out of the equation, why not? "I leave in eight days."

His eyes were hot enough to melt her before he turned away and chipped at a paint stain on the ladder.

Yes or no? She wasn't going to ask. "You did a nice job with the paint touch-ups, and the windows sparkle. Fran's Valentine's Day guests are sure to be impressed."

Months ago, a couple eager to spend the holiday weekend here had reserved the Orca Suite. For that matter, every room in the Oceanside was booked.

"This suite is always rented."

"That's understandable—this is a place for lovers."

Lovers. The word hung between them.

Nick swallowed. "With every room here booked over the Valentine's Day weekend, where will you stay?"

"I'm moving into Fran's spare bedroom tomorrow. After the guests check out the following Monday and the room is cleaned, I'll move back here."

He nodded and positioned the ladder.

"I'm going downstairs now. I'll leave you in peace."

"Peace?" He glanced at his erection and let out a low laugh. "Not this morning. I have a lot on my plate today."

No sex today, then. Disappointed, she headed down the stairs.

STANDING ON THE middle step of the ladder, Nick unscrewed the fan and took it from the ceiling. Instead of mulling over the repairs he needed to make, he thought about loving Cinnamon. In front of the fire, in bed, against the wall. He almost dropped the fan. Forget sex, he needed to do his job without breaking the thing.

He finished without a hitch, then went right back to wanting Cinnamon. As soon as he checked to make sure the fan worked, he'd pack up and head downstairs to find her.

Chapter Twenty

CINNAMON WAS CURLED up in a large armchair, a comfy place to read. The thriller she'd chosen promised to grab her attention, but no such luck. Over the last hour she'd read the first three pages several times. She may as well have been reading the phonebook. Knowing Nick was upstairs made concentrating impossible.

How long could fixing a fan take? Restless and edgy, she tossed the book aside and stood.

She needed to distract herself, and doing the factory projections would help. She'd go to the factory after all, where she could forget her longing and focus. First she needed her laptop and purse, which were both in the suite.

With butterflies in her stomach she headed up the stairs. *Don't be silly. It won't happen today. He has too much to do.*

When she entered the suite the fan was making lazy

circles, gently stirring the air. Nick's arm looped around the ladder. "You can have your room back. I'm done. The fan works great."

"Fran will be happy."

The casual conversation calmed her down. With a relieved sigh she headed into the bedroom and retrieved her purse from the dresser. Slinging it over her shoulder, she moved to the desk, to get the laptop. "I've decidcd to work at the factory."

"Dressed like that?"

Frowning, she set down her things to check the zipper of her jeans—closed—and smooth her dove-gray sweater over her hips. "Is there something wrong with my clothes?"

"Not a thing, but you usually dress up when you work."

"You think I should change into something nicer before I go?"

"I think you look great no matter what you wear."

The naked hunger on his face fueled the fever she was trying to contain. She couldn't look away, couldn't stop the soft moan that slipped from her lips.

"Sharon says," he started. Stopped and cleared his throat. "She says you, Vince, and Drake met with a lawyer about the employee buyout."

"That's right." She managed a casual nod at odds with her thudding heart. "A buyout is definitely doable. It's complicated. But the way I understand it, employees will buy into the company using part of each paycheck to purchase shares. The bank will be involved with financing. We're meeting with everyone tomorrow to answer questions and vote. Then the company attorney will take the offer to Tate's attorney."

"Sounds good. Everyone appreciates what you're doing."

"I'm happy with our progress. Yesterday I had a phone interview with a consulting company in Boston."

"And?"

"I don't know—I need that job, but I really like it here." I really like you, Nick.

His blazing eyes dipped to her mouth, but the frustrating man didn't make a move to kiss her again or anything else. What was he waiting for?

Forget that. She moistened her lips with her tongue and lowered her eyelids.

"What the hell?"

"I don't care if you have other jobs today, Nick. I swear to God, if you don't seduce me right now, I'll seduce you."

Before she could chicken out she pulled her sweater

over her head and moved toward him, straight into his arms. He kissed her like he was dying of thirst and she was water. She lost herself in sensation and need. Somehow they moved to the bedroom and the bed, and her bra disappeared.

She lay on her back. He kissed her mouth, her neck, then did delicious things to her breasts. When she was wild with hunger and desperate for more, he slid his hand down her stomach and unbuttoned her jeans. She raised her hips and silently begged him to go lower.

"Easy," he cautioned, bracing his weight on his elbows.

"I want you, Nick."

He let out the low laugh. "And I want you naked."

He stripped off her jeans and panties. Then sat back and studied her. "You are so beautiful."

"That's nice, but I need more than words."

"Is that right." He teased and stroked her everywhere except the place she most wanted attention. She wished he'd take off his clothes, but the haze of desire clouded her brain. If he didn't touch her there, she'd die. She pushed his hand lower. "Please, Nick, I need you."

"Here?"

He slipped his hand between her legs and finally put his fingers on her. Inside her. A moan filled the air. Hers, she realized.

"You're slick and wet."

"You did that, you clever man." She pulled his head down and kissed him with all the passion she'd bottled up since the day in her office.

Whimpering, she writhed against his magic hand.

"Is that good?"

"Yes." Breathing hard she stilled. "It's been awhile and I'm afraid… I mean… I'm close to—"

"Climaxing? Let it happen, Cinn."

She *felt* like sin. "What about you?" she managed, his skilled fingers making it difficult to form the words.

"Not this time. This is for you."

Her eyelids drifted closed. He knew exactly how to touch her, deepening her hunger until her entire focus was on his fingers and the spiraling tension inside. Crying out, she let go and flew apart.

When she drifted back to earth she drew in a shuddering breath and smiled. "Mmm."

"Yeah. I enjoyed it too. Watching you come is such a turn on."

She was too content to feel embarrassed.

But it wasn't fair that he was still dressed. She sat up and gestured for him to do the same. He gave her a questioning look, but did it. Wordless, she worked the buttons of his shirt, pausing to caress his chest. Beneath her hand his heart pounded. She pushed the soft flannel off his shoulders and tossed the shirt aside. Ran her hands over his broad shoulders and down his solid chest. He was perfect, hard and muscled and beautiful.

She wanted him inside her.

On her knees now, clasping his shoulders she licked his nipples, mimicking what he'd done to her. He groaned, and she smiled to herself. She kissed his rib cage, then his navel. He sucked in a breath and went still.

As she reached for his zipper, he grasped her wrist and stopped her.

"Better not." Breathing hard, he rolled out of reach.

This was the second time he'd stopped.

"Why not?" Puzzled, and suddenly embarrassed at her nudity, Cinnamon wriggled under the covers. She pulled up the comforter, tucking it under her armpits. "Is it me?"

While Nick retrieved his shirt from the floor, she leaned against the hard wooden headboard. He shook his head, then shrugged into his shirt. "You're amazing."

"Then is it a religious thing, or do you have a disease?"

He almost smiled. "Neither. I don't think making love is a good idea."

Totally confused, she gaped at him. "I don't understand. Earlier you said… We talked about seduction. I understand you're really busy today, but I thought… We've gone this far, and we're both single and unattached, so why not?"

"For starters, I don't have birth control with me."

Was that all? "That's okay. I'm on the pill."

She gave him a hopeful glance. But he muttered something under his breath. "What did you say?" she asked.

"This is more complicated than birth control." He propped himself against the headboard beside her.

"I've been tested for all the diseases. I'm clean."

"Same, but that's not what I'm talking about. You're an educated executive and I'm a handyman," he said as he rebuttoned his shirt. "We're not a good fit."

A similar argument to the one Cinnamon had told herself. But she no longer believed it. "A few minutes ago we seemed to fit fine. We share a strong attraction we can't seem to fight. And you're far more than a handyman. You're a gifted inventor with a talent for fixing almost anything."

"Believe what you want." He waved off the compliments, the same as always. "There are things you don't know about me."

"I'm pretty open-minded," she coaxed, touching his cheek. "Try me."

Pain and doubt filled his eyes before he pulled away from her. He crossed his arms, and his mouth set in a stubborn line. He wasn't going to confide in her.

Stifling a frustrated sigh, she tried again. "Keep your secrets, then. You're a good man, a loving uncle and brother, and a loyal friend. That's enough for me."

He hesitated, and she pressed her case. "We're adults, and we're heading into this with our eyes open. No promises and no commitments, if that's what's stopping you. Just really great sex." She aimed a pointed glance at his erection. "Besides, if you don't get some relief soon, you're liable to explode," she teased.

He lightened up a bit. "There are other ways to take care of that. Despite what you say, you're not a 'just sex' woman, Cinnamon."

"Oh, no? Why do you think I left my last job?" She didn't want to share the sordid past, and wished she'd kept her mouth shut. But she had Nick's full attention. If talking about what happened helped convince him to make love with her, the story was worth the telling.

That didn't mean she could look at him while she told it. She picked a feather from the down quilt. "Dwight Sabin, a founding partner of Sabin and Howe, was separated from his wife. We had an affair. Then he went back to her," she finished, leaving out the rest. "So you see, I know about sex without commitment."

There, it was out. She pulled in a fortifying breath before meeting his gaze. "Now you know my dirty little secret."

For one long moment she thought she'd convinced him. A tender expression warmed his face, and he brushed the bangs from her forehead. "So that's why you resigned. Were you in love with the guy?"

"At the time I thought so, but now I realize I was flattered. To have a big shot like Dwight Sabin interested in me gave me quite a swelled head." She sighed. "Until people started talking about me as if I'd lured him into bed and schemed to destroy his marriage, all for a promotion...." The indignity of it hit her in the stomach, and she felt sick. "I couldn't stay there."

"I'm real sorry for what happened to you, but your story confirms what I suspected—you need more from a man than sex. You deserve that." Nick stroked her cheek. "If I could, I'd deck the bastard for hurting you that way. What I can do is leave you alone, so I don't hurt you too." He rose from the bed. "Tell Fran I'll be back next week, after the tourists clear out."

LYING IN BED that night, miserable and rock hard with

need, Nick wondered at his stupidity. He'd had the chance to live his fantasies and make love with Cinnamon, and what had he done? Turned her down.

You're a good man, a loving uncle and brother, and a loyal friend. That's enough for me.

Words that flattered and tempted him, but he knew better. He was small potatoes, not high-powered enough for Cinnamon. She deserved a man who loved her and who could give her security and plenty of money. Nick didn't fit that bill by a long shot.

She claimed she wanted him, but if she knew he could barely read, she'd change her mind so fast… He winced at the thought.

"So tell her and solve your problem," he grumbled into the darkness.

But he knew he never would. He couldn't bear to see her pity. Or worse, know that she thought him stupid.

The best thing for her was to hook up with a hotshot executive—as long as he didn't use her the way her jerk of a boss had.

From now on Nick would do his lusting for her in private. If it killed him he wouldn't touch her again. His cock pulsed painfully. It probably would kill him.

Swearing and desperate to clear his brain, he turned to the only possible relief, unsatisfying as it was. Self-gratification.

Chapter Twenty-One

HAVING SETTLED INTO the spare bedroom of Fran's apartment in the basement of the Oceanside after dinner, Cinnamon and her friend sat on the sofa, sharing a bowl of popcorn.

"Here we are, just like college." Cinnamon wiped her buttery fingers on her napkin and glanced around the cozy living room. "Only this is a whole lot nicer than any dorm room."

"But just as much fun." Fran gave Cinnamon a probing look. "What's bothering you?"

"How did you know?"

"You're about to shred that poor napkin to bits. That happens when your hands get restless, and that's a sure sign you're troubled."

"You know me too well." Cinnamon lobbed the napkin into the wastebasket a few feet away. "Would you care to guess who?"

"Nick."

"Uh-huh."

"Did something happen when he stopped by to fix the fan yesterday?"

And how, thanks to his excellent kissing and red hot hands. She'd touched heaven. "Yes and no. I'm pretty frustrated."

Fran nodded, but didn't pry. She never had. "If you want to talk about it, I'm here."

How to admit that the man you wanted desperately refused to make love with you? Cinnamon toyed with the half-empty popcorn bowl. "He claims there are things I don't know about him," she hedged. "Whatever they are, they're powerful enough to keep us apart."

Fran's eyes narrowed. "Secrets, huh?" She shook her head. "This is the first I've heard of any, but I suppose we all have one or two."

"Then you don't know what he meant? I hoped you did." Cinnamon released a defeated sigh. "Well, I guess that's that."

"Don't bet on it. There's always the Valentine's Day dance. Music, champagne punch, a romantic atmosphere…" She fiddled with the gold stud in her ear. "A sexy dress might help, and spiky 'love me' heels. Jamie's Boutique off Main Street is a good place to shop for both."

"I don't know. What if it doesn't work?"

"Then you still have a hot new outfit."

"Ooh, I can't resist that." She really shouldn't spend the money, but with the Boston job a definite possibility… For the first time all day, Cinnamon smiled. "We need to figure out when to shop, and with the dance in two days we don't have much time. "I have that factory meeting at Town Hall tomorrow afternoon, and you'll be busy with your guests, so that's out. But we could shop in the morning, before we meet the Friday girls for lunch. Can you go after breakfast?"

Fran grinned. "As soon as I clean up the kitchen."

As soon as Cinnamon left the Friday girls lunch, Fran gestured her friends forward. She needed to get back to the Oceanside to greet her guests, but this was important.

"Can you keep a secret?" All five women nodded. "Just for an hour, until everyone at Town Hall knows."

"So this is about Cinnamon and the cranberry factory," Betsy mused, a valid assumption, as that was where Cinnamon was headed for the buyout meeting.

Fran nodded. "You're going to like this—if you swear to keep it to yourselves," she repeated, looking each woman in the eye.

Betsy pretended to turn a key over her lips. Claire and Lynn nodded solemnly, and Joelle and Noelle crossed their hearts.

About to top off the coffees, Andie stopped. "Should I come back in a minute?"

Fran shook her head. "You'll want to hear this too."

The restaurant owner signaled the other waitresses to take care of her station, then pulled an empty chair over and sat down.

Bursting with excitement, Fran forced herself to speak in a voice that wouldn't carry. "I spoke with the mayor this morning, and guess what? Tate agreed to the employee buyout. They're going to offer Cinnamon a job as general manager of the factory."

"Wahoo!" Andie's fist shot into the air. Everyone seemed equally delighted.

"I don't know if she'll accept the job," Fran cautioned. "But I do know she really likes Nick. Apparently he's sending her mixed messages. If we want her to stay, we have to do something about that."

"What is he, blind?" Joelle said.

Betsy looked puzzled. "I saw how he looked at her at the town meeting last week. He's interested, all right. I thought—I mean, she said she didn't want him."

"She's changed her mind," Fran said.

"Does Nick know that?"

"I don't know—wish I'd thought to ask. According to Cinnamon, he claims there are 'things' she doesn't know about him."

They all looked as clueless as Fran was.

Andie shrugged. "Whatever they are, they can't be so bad. Nick is one of the nicest guys I know. He's darn cute, too." She chuckled. "If I were Cinnamon's age, I'd be after him in a Dunlin Shores second."

"Amen, sister," Betsy agreed. "If I wasn't in love with my husband."

"Anyway," Fran said, "whatever these 'things' are, they've stopped any romance from developing. But take heart. Sharon phoned me the other day to discuss this very thing. She says even though Nick doesn't talk about Cinnamon, he definitely is attracted to and interested in her."

"Didn't I just say the same thing?" Betsy said.

"You did, but there's a problem," Fran went on. "Nick isn't acknowledging his feelings. He may not even realize how much he cares about Cinnamon. Sharon says he needs a push, and that's where we come in. This morning I went shopping with Cinnamon for a dress and shoes for tomorrow night's dance. Wait'll you see the her. Her outfit should knock Nick's socks off. But we need something more."

The women were silent a moment, each pondering the situation.

"I know." Joelle brightened. "We'll ask the band to play lots of slow, romantic songs and make sure—"

"They dance together," Noelle finished.

"Keep the lights dim," Andie added. "That adds a romantic air to things. And the band should make each song last a long time. I can picture Cinnamon and Nick now, dancing slow and holding each other close…" She sighed. "Makes my heart go pity-pat."

Dreamy nods all around.

"And don't let anyone cut in when they're dancing," Betsy said. She looked thoughtful. "Better yet, make sure some other good-looking guy goes after Cinnamon. To make Nick jealous."

Andie nodded. "That's bound to work."

Such great ideas. Fran beamed. "I knew we'd come up with something."

Chapter Twenty-Two

EVEN BEFORE CINNAMON reached the dining room for Saturday breakfast, she heard laughter and conversation from Fran's guests. They sounded happy, but with Fran's warmth and delicious food, who wouldn't be?

Cinnamon wasn't as outgoing, but she was hungry. She also needed to talk with her friend. They'd both been busy and hadn't seen each other since lunch yesterday. Cinnamon had exchanged several texts with her about her surprising job offer from the factory, but Fran didn't know about the call from the consulting company in Boston. A high-salaried position was hers if she wanted it.

Two offers! Talk about a much needed morale booster. Regardless which position she chose, she could buy something at the art show without worrying about the money.

"Here she is at last." Fran smiled. "This is Cinnamon

Smith, the friend I've been telling you about," she told the couples grouped around the table. "She came in too late last night to meet you then, because she was being wined and dined by our mayor and his wife. I heard about that in a text."

Fran turned to Cinnamon. "I had to get up at four to cook for you all, and I'm anxious to know, but you'll tell me later. Now for the introductions." She gestured to one side of the table, which she'd extended with an extra leaf. "Cinnamon, meet Mitch, who has come every year for four years, and his lady friend, Carin. They're in the Orca Suite. Next to them, Mark and Megan, Stephanie and Anthony, and Kirk and Elise. Across the table, Jim and Sue, who are celebrating their second Valentine's Day with us, Jess and Tina, back after a stay over the Fourth of July, and Bo and Carol." She blew out a breath. "Whew!"

Everyone laughed, Cinnamon included.

"I'll never remember all your names, but hi." Cinnamon sat in the lone empty seat beside Sue. She gestured at the gulls on the railing outside. "Did Fran tell you about Stubby and Stumpy?"

"First thing this morning," Mitch replied. "Carin has flipped over them."

His female companion nodded. "Mitch mentioned

the gulls on the drive down, but I didn't realize how adorable they are."

"And they know it." Fran brought Cinnamon a steaming mug of coffee. "The second batch of rolls will be out of the oven shortly. Meanwhile, help yourself to quiche, ham, and bacon." Her eyes sparkled and she seemed to glow with happiness at the table filled with guests. "And of course, cranberry juice."

"We heard about that, too, and dutifully drank the stuff. Not my favorite, but I wanted to do my part," quipped one of the men whose name Cinnamon didn't recall.

While everyone ate and chatted, Cinnamon studied the people around her. Maybe it was the soft classical music and cozy fire crackling in the great room, or the view, or Valentine's Day weekend, but each couple seemed engrossed in each other—including the man and woman who she assumed were in their sixties. Everyone made polite conversation, but the intimate looks couples exchanged and the way they leaned into each other left no doubt about what was on each of their minds. Love and sex.

Cinnamon dropped her gaze to her place. As the only woman at the table without a partner, she definitely stuck out. Not that she minded being alone. She didn't need a man to be content. In a show of independence she popped a forkful of quiche into her mouth, straightened her shoulders, and held her chin high.

Yet inside, she felt hollow. Maybe she didn't need a man, but she wanted one in particular. Nick Mahoney.

"Now that everyone is here, let me wish you a happy Valentine's Day," Fran said. "I hope you're all planning to stroll around the Love on Main Street outdoor art show sometime today. Many of our local artists are selling some great stuff there. And please, come to the dance tonight. Both events are fun. By the way, we serve great food at the dance. Including chocolate."

Lots of chuckling.

Sue and her husband smiled at each other and linked hands. "Fran's right. Last year we went to both and had a wonderful time. We met quite a few of the locals, which was interesting."

Fran nodded. "Tonight we're honoring Abby Mahoney, our star twelve-year-old, who won the Oregon State math bee in her age category. She lives right here in town."

While the guests talked about that phenomenon, Cinnamon thought about the evening ahead—and Nick. Yesterday Fran had helped her find a slinky dress and a pair of four-inch heels, but that was no guarantee he'd care. Even if he was attracted to her, he could reject her again.

That frustrating possibility loomed over her head like a dark rain cloud, and she considered staying in and reading a book instead. But she wanted to applaud Abby. And if she accepted the job in Boston, this could be her last chance to see Nick and the people she'd grown so fond of.

Sue tore her gaze from her husband to focus on Cinnamon. "Fran says you're a consultant," she said, while Jim continued to shower his wife with mooney-eyed love.

Envy sliced through Cinnamon. Would a man— Nick in particular—ever look at her that way? "That's right," she replied, picking at a slice of ham.

The couple across from her shared a quick but tender kiss that left her feeling even more bereft.

Why in the world had she sat down to breakfast with this group of lovers? No longer hungry, she wondered how to leave without seeming rude.

"A very talented consultant," Fran added from the kitchen. "Over the past few weeks Cinnamon helped orchestrate an employee buyout of our cranberry factory that will save the company from going under."

"Really," Mitch said, and others offered impressed

murmurs.

Cinnamon gave a modest shrug. "I didn't do it alone. I had plenty of help."

"Maybe so," Fran conceded as she brought the coffeepot in for refills. "But nothing would have happened without you. And that's not all," she added. "Yesterday the factory offered her a job as general manager. The whole town hopes she'll take it. That's why the mayor and his wife treated her to dinner last night."

Cinnamon shot her big-mouth friend a how-dare-you-tell-these-strangers frown. Ignoring her, Fran returned the coffeepot to the kitchen.

"A job right here in town. I'd love to live here," one of the others said.

Having popped a mouthful of quiche into her mouth, Cinnamon chewed slowly, giving herself time to form a reply. She also loved the town, and enjoyed seeing a lot of Fran and getting to know her new friends. The challenge of running the factory definitely excited her.

The salary wasn't as much as what the firm in Boston offered, but the cost of living here was less expensive. To sweeten the pot, Mayor Jannings had thrown in lots of perks, including an ocean-front, rent-to-own home, and the promise that once the company turned a profit, her pay would rise accordingly, with bonuses as well.

The one drawback was Nick. Lust aside, she was falling for him, which scared her half to death. He wasn't interested in settling down. She wasn't sure she wanted that either, not with Nick. At least, that's what she told herself.

Could she live in a town where she was sure to bump into him often. Would she have trouble forgetting him and moving on with her life? She longed to discuss her doubts with Fran, but with so many guests this weekend, the talk would have to wait.

Her tablemates were expecting her reply. "The offer came as a huge surprise. I'm flattered and interested, but I haven't made up my mind." May as well tell the group and Fran about Boston. "The funny thing is, I also got a job offer from a consulting group in Boston.

Fran raised her eyebrows. "You didn't mention that. Congratulations," she said with zero enthusiasm.

"It happened late yesterday afternoon, and we haven't seen each other."

"I suppose you'll be taking that position?"

Two weeks ago, Cinnamon would've answered 'yes' without hesitation. Now she sighed. "I honestly don't know. They're giving me a full week to make up my mind."

"You have some serious decisions to make," Mitch

observed.

Everyone at the table went silent—the perfect opportunity to leave.

The kitchen timer buzzed. "The second batch of breakfast rolls is ready." Fran turned toward the kitchen.

Cinnamon glanced out the window, where patches of blue sky were visible. "I'm going to take a beach walk and do some thinking. I'll see you all later."

NICK HATED DANCES, especially this one. Standing near the stage at Town Hall, he tugged at his tie, which felt too tight, and noted the endless hearts papering the walls. Above the stage, red and purple garlands draped a huge "Happy Valentine's Day" heart. Beneath it, band members set up.

Love. Who needed it? By the huge crowd gathered here, everyone. Except him. Feeling like the Valentine's Day Scrooge, he scowled.

Until Finn Brannigan, photographer for the digital and print versions of the Dunlin Shores News Weekly, pointed his camera Nick's way. Nick forced a big smile. Finn had taken several photos of Abby for the paper, and no doubt wanted pictures of locals and tourists for the same reason.

Everyone wore fancy clothes, including Cinnamon. Between the sparkly red dress hugging her curves and the do-me heels setting off her sexy legs, his eyes about popped out of his head. He wasn't the only one. Every male in the place checked her out. That pissed him off.

He gave a couple of them warning looks, and they glanced away. Much better. As if he had any business feeling protective or jealous. He had no claim on her. He hadn't seen her since the day he'd fixed the fan, and he meant to steer clear of her tonight as well. It was the only way to stay out of trouble.

After Abby accepted her award, locals clustered around her, Cinnamon among them. Like a tomcat around catnip, Nick started toward her. Vince and two other guys from the factory pulled his attention away to talk about this and that. By the time he got rid of them, Cinnamon had disappeared.

Well, hell. Where had she gone?

He'd heard about her two job offers. Everyone had. Which one would she take? If she stuck around town, he'd never get her out of his system. In a rotten mood, he approached his sister. "I'm outta here."

For some reason looking panicky, she clasped his arm. "You can't leave yet. You have to dance with Abby."

Nick eyed his niece, one of half a dozen twelve-year-old females giggling and chattering away. From time to time they shot sly glances at the group of awkward boys hovering nearby.

Nick sized up the boys. If any of them so much as touched his niece… But they looked scared half to death, and he figured she was safe. "It's not me she wants to dance with," he grumbled.

Sharon laughed. "Then dance with me, so I don't look like a total misfit."

"I don't think you have to worry about that." Nick nodded toward the refreshment table. "Drake Jessup's been checking you out since he walked in."

"Has he?"

To his surprise his sister blushed. "When did that happen?" he asked.

"As yet, nothing has happened, but I wouldn't mind. Look at Liz, over by the band."

Nick spotted her, hanging on some poor tourist's arm, a flirty grin on her face.

"Looks as if she won't be bothering you tonight," Sharon observed.

"Thank God for small favors. Drake's not as bold as his older sister."

"That's okay." Sharon fluffed her hair. "I think I'll get myself a cup of punch. Wish me luck."

Nick watched her go, noting that Drake straightened his shoulders and smoothed down his hair. His sister and Drake. He shook his head. He'd never have guessed.

Ready to leave, he turned toward the exit. A sparkly red dress snagged his attention. Cinnamon.

Damn.

She was near the exit, talking with Fran, Joelle, Noelle, and Andie. If he wanted to leave, he'd have to pass the whole nosy group. Muttering, he shoved his hands in his pockets and headed forward. Andie nudged Fran, and all the women waved. Before he reached them they melted into the crowd. Except for Cinnamon, who stood waiting for him.

Which made him nervous, although he couldn't have said why. And why was he fighting a grin?

"Hi," she smiled as he sauntered up. "I saw you earlier, but it's crowded in here and people wanted to chat, and I lost you."

"Seems like this dance gets bigger every year. Nice dress."

"Thanks. You look good yourself. A sports coat and tie, dress pants—you clean up well."

"Don't expect to see me this way again. I only dress up for special occasions. I did this for Abby."

"Aww, that's sweet. Presenting her with a plaque and

a savings bond, and having her picture taken for the paper—such a cool way to applaud her talent."

"The whole town is proud of her." He'd said hello, now he could leave. But his feet disagreed, and he stayed right where he was. "I spoke with the patent attorney yesterday. She filed seven patents for me."

"That many? You're amazing. By the way, you should be getting a check from the cranberry factory soon for those repairs. Royalties will follow. I have a hunch that's just the beginning."

Sure would be nice. He wouldn't have to worry about paying Abby's camp expenses. He grinned. "Thanks to you."

"You did the work. I only planted the idea."

The lights dimmed and the band started a low, sultry number. "Dance with me," he said, surprising himself.

"Okay." She moved into place and clasped his shoulder.

"That's not how I dance." Nick wrapped his arms around her waist and cinched her nice and close. She twined her arms around his neck, and he nodded. "Much better."

In her heels, the top of her head almost reached his chin. Her perfume filled his senses. "You smell good," he said, enjoying the feel of her soft curves against him.

She smiled up at him. "I hoped you'd like it."

She had? That stopped him. "Everyone is talking about your two job offers. Which one are you going to take?"

She shook her head. "News sure travels fast."

"That's Dunlin Shores for you." Someone bumped into him and he danced her toward the corner, where it was less crowded. "Nobody knows which job you'll take, though," he said, pulling back to look at her.

"I haven't made up my mind yet."

Tonight her lips were fire-engine red, matching the dress, and he couldn't tear his eyes away. He wanted badly to kiss her.

"I'm thinking about making a list of pros and cons for each job to help me decide," she said.

His cock was rock-hard now. Surely she felt it against her stomach. He cleared his throat. "That sounds like something you'd do."

"How would you decide?" she asked, snuggling closer.

He started to slide his hands to her ass, but there were too many people around. One signal from her and he'd take her home and make love with her, consequences be damned.

Someone tapped his shoulder. Nick turned his head

to find Claude standing there.

"Mind if I cut in?" he asked, a sly look on his face.

What was that about?

"Yeah, I do," Nick growled.

Claude shrugged and grinned. "Can't fault a guy for trying." He jerked his chin at two others from the factory. "A couple of my buddies want a chance to dance with her."

"They're out of luck." At Nick's narrowed eyes, they shifted nervously.

"I like a man who knows what he wants. Can you guess what I want?" She touched her tongue to her upper lip.

Nick stifled a groan. "Don't tempt me. Being inside you is all I can think of, but I don't want to hurt you like your ex did."

"The only way that'll happen is if you turn me down again. Then, I just might self-combust."

"Wouldn't want that to happen." Bending low he placed his mouth against her ear. "Let's get out of here."

Chapter Twenty-Three

A S SOON AS Nick pulled the truck into his carport and shut off the ignition, he exited the cab. In the sudden silence Cinnamon's thudding heart seemed so loud she was sure the entire neighborhood heard it.

An instant later he grasped her waist and helped her out. Surrounded by the murmur of the ocean and the salty tang of the sea air, she wrapped her arms around him and slid down his hard body.

He took her lips—no, possessed them—with an urgency that inflamed her already needy body. Liquid heat raced through her and settled in her female parts. Clinging to him, she returned the kiss.

After a while, his breathing ragged, he tore his mouth from hers. "Let's go inside."

Grabbing her hand, he hurried her up the stone walkway toward the door. Despite the cold, his fingers were warm.

A full, silvery moon peeked through the clouds and

reflected brightly on the water. In a daze, she stared at the sight. "You never said you lived on the ocean."

"This place isn't much—it's a beach bungalow." He sounded apologetic.

"I don't care about that." Standing in the glow of the porch light while Nick unlocked the door, she stared at the moon's reflection on the water. "Such a beautiful setting."

Nick opened the door and turned to her. "You're beautiful. And I want you so much."

Standing in the threshold of his house, he kissed her again. This time with a tender sweetness that left her panting for more. He pulled her inside. She glimpsed a small living room lit by a table lamp before he kicked the door shut, tugged her coat off, and tossed it on the sofa.

His tie followed, landing someplace. Then his sports coat. He unbuttoned his shirt, his glittering eyes on her. "You look so hot in that outfit."

"When you look at me like that, I feel hot. Touch me." Cinnamon guided his hands to her aching breasts.

With a deep male growl, he kissed her again. Then broke away. "I want you out of that dress. Turn around."

His fingers shook as he tugged the zipper down—or was she the one trembling? She pivoted toward him and shimmied out of the dress, showing off her demi bra, bikini panties, and thigh high stockings.

If his eyes got any hotter, the whole room would burst into flames. "Have mercy."

"Not tonight." She reached for him. After more kisses and lots of fondling, she was going up in flames. "Make love with me."

"The bedroom is this way." He lifted her in his arms and started down a narrow hall.

They didn't get far before he stopped to kiss her. Along the way her bra disappeared, along with his shirt.

"Forget the bed." He set her down and pushed her against the wall. She wrapped her thighs around his hips, and he thrust against her. A picture nearby fell off the wall and crashed to the floor.

"Oops," she said. "I think your bed might be safer."

"We'll see about that." He carried her into the bed-room.

Light from the hall spilled into the otherwise dark room. Ignoring the bedspread, he tumbled her onto the mattress. "As sexy as those panties and stockings are, they have to go."

"Same with your pants."

"Yours first. Lie down." Cinnamon closed her eyes and savored the most sensual foreplay of her life, as Nick slowly peeled off her stockings and panties, stopping to kiss her newly bared inner thighs with soft, whiskery kisses.

The mattress dipped as he joined her. Kissing her face, her neck, her breasts, licking and suckling until she writhed under him.

"You seem to like this."

"Quit talking and keep going."

Wicked grin. "Plan on it. Just you wait."

He nudged her thighs further apart and tasted his wicked way down her body. Aching with anticipation, she trembled.

Prolonged attention to her tender inner thighs heightened the agony. Whimpering with need, she finally felt his hot breath where she most wanted it. His mouth, his fingers…

Pleasure spiraled through her, sending her higher and higher. Teetering on the edge of control, she pulled back. "My turn. Take off your shorts and lie down."

"Yes, ma'am."

He was as perfect as she'd imagined, all hard muscle. His penis jutted out, huge and magnificent. Swallowing, she traced his length with her fingers.

Suddenly he clasped her wrist. "Keep that up and I'll embarrass myself." He flipped her onto her back and poised himself over her. "Are you ready?"

"So ready." She wrapped her thighs around his hips.

One thrust and he was deep inside her. He stilled. "I went in a little fast. Too much?"

Shuddering pleasure pulsed through her. "Just right." Focused body and soul on Nick, she squeezed him with her inner muscles. "Do that again."

"Like this?" He thrust.

She'd thought he was in deep before, but somehow he went deeper. "That's good," she whispered. "Very good. Don't stop."

"Right." He shifted a little and moved exactly the way she needed. As her climax built, he joined her in an orgasm so intense her world broke apart.

When she came back to earth, she was sprawled beside him, her head on his chest and his arm around her. Under her ear his heart beat furiously, the fast but steady rhythm somehow reassuring. She felt warm and full, and for the first time in her life, whole.

She loved him.

Nick had been right—she wasn't a "just sex" woman. Frightened by the intensity of her feelings, she struggled to untangle herself.

"Come back here, you." He nuzzled her shoulder and pulled her closer. "You are so sexy."

Which was good. Too bad he didn't want love to go

with the sex. He wouldn't be happy if he found out she'd given him her heart. She wasn't about to let on.

"You're not so bad yourself." Masking her feelings, she lifted her head and smiled in a performance worthy of an Oscar.

She ought to leave now, before she did something foolish and ruined everything by blurting out her feelings. She opened her mouth to tell him she wanted to go.

"I'm thinking," he said, his brown eyes as warm as melted chocolate. "We ought to make love again, to see how we do the second time." His hand slipped between her legs.

Desire melted her resolve, and her common sense along with it. She could no more leave than stop breathing. She arched into his touch. "I like the way you think."

SATED AND AT peace, Nick nestled Cinnamon closer and kissed the top of her head. "The second time was every bit as hot as the first. We're great in bed."

"Mmm," she mumbled, sounding as if she were almost asleep.

Drowsy himself, Nick adjusted the covers and closed

his eyes. He liked lying here with Cinnamon. He liked the smell of sex and woman and the feel of her soft behind under his palm.

Warm breath slipped from her lips, fanning his chest. Shifting, she looped her leg over his thighs. Just like that he wanted her again.

And here he'd thought once or twice would take care of his hunger for her. Nope, he wanted her more than ever.

As if she'd heard his thoughts and seconded the feeling, she kissed his chest. Chuckling softly, he slid his hand to her breast.

She made the throaty sound he liked. "I love you, Nick."

Words that scared him spitless. "No, you don't."

Untangling his arms and legs, he sat up. He turned on the bedside lamp, blinking in the stark light.

Looking every bit as frightened, Cinnamon followed him up, pulling the covers with her. Leaning against the headboard, she tucked the blanket under her armpits.

"I never meant to fall in love with you, but to-night..." Her fingers fretted with the blanket, smoothing it needlessly. "I wasn't going to say it, but I was half-asleep and the words slipped out. I can't help how I feel, Nick, and I can't lie about it either. I love you."

Dazzled by her statement, he basked in the knowledge for one bright moment. Until a voice in his head cautioned him. *Get real. If she finds out you read like a five-year old…*

He couldn't go there. He wouldn't tell her, not now. Not ever.

"I'm not asking you to love me back," she said, her cinnamon eyes looking straight into his soul.

That was a relief. Unable to bear those searching eyes one more second, he jerked his attention to the clock on the bedside table. "It's two in the morning—time I took you back to the Oceanside."

He swung his legs over the bed and stood. Cinnamon's panties were on the floor, a vivid speck of red on the beige carpet. Averting his eyes he tossed them onto the bed. Her bra and dress were someplace else—the living room or hall. He padded from the bedroom, retrieved them and brought them to her.

"Shouldn't we talk?" she asked, still clutching the blanket to her naked body.

"Not now. I need my rest and so do you."

He turned his back while she dressed. Grabbed his boxers from the floor and stepped into them. Ignoring his dress clothes, he pulled clean jeans and a T-shirt from his dresser.

Fully clothed, he faced her. "Let's go."

Perched on his bed, wearing her bra and panties but not the dress, with her arms folded and legs stretched in front of her and crossed at the ankle, she shook her head. "Not until you tell me what you're afraid of."

What the hell? "I'm not scared of anything." A big, fat lie.

"Prove it. Tell me what you're hiding."

With her jaw set in determination and the fiery glint in her eyes, any fool could see she wasn't going anyplace until she got some kind of explanation.

Suddenly tired, he sat down on the lone chair, well out of reach of the bed. Scrubbing his hand over his face, he searched for something that would get her off his case. Anything but the real reason.

"You deserve better than me," he said at last. Which was God's honest truth.

For several long seconds she stared at him, wanting more. Matching her body language he crossed his arms and clamped his jaw.

Finally she threw up her hands. "You win, Nick." She jerked the dress over her head. "Take me home."

Chapter Twenty-Four

LATE SUNDAY AFTERNOON, relieved that Fran's last guest had checked out, Cinnamon propped her sock-covered feet on the ottoman and sipped her wine. "How does it feel to have an almost empty house again?"

"Don't get me wrong," Fran said as she coaxed a smoldering log into flames in the great room. "I thoroughly enjoy taking care of my guests, but after all that work organizing and setting up for the art show and the dance, plus serving huge breakfasts in the morning and wine and cheese in the afternoons, the peace and quiet is a welcome break."

"They were a nice, friendly group of people," Cinnamon agreed. "But I like having you all to myself again."

"I feel the same way." Brushing her hands together, Fran moved from the fireplace to the long sofa. With a sigh she sank down next to Cinnamon. "I'm ready to relax and wait for that pizza we ordered. So keep the wine flowing and tell me everything."

No need to ask what she meant. Everyone from the clerk at the grocery to the recently departed guests seemed to know Cinnamon had gone home last night with Nick.

But no one knew about her frustration or her broken heart.

After a restless night—what had been left of it—and a full day of silent brooding over last night's disaster with Nick, she needed to talk about it. "It's not good."

The anticipatory gleam faded from her friend's eyes. "You mean he's lousy in bed?"

The only thing to do was laugh. "Actually, he's quite good."

And then some. Despite her broken heart, her well-loved body still purred with satisfaction.

"But?"

Cinnamon stretched her toes toward the fire, savoring the warmth. "I'm in love with him."

"That's wonderful! Is that why you're so glum— because you fell for Nick instead of an executive?"

"I don't care about that anymore. Not that it matters. He isn't in love with me."

Her friend shot her an incredulous look. "After the way he looked at you at the dance and refused to let

ANN ROTH

anyone cut in, I find that hard to believe."

"Believe it." How else to explain his less-than-thrilled reaction when she'd told him and his unwillingness to talk? He'd hustled her out of his bed and house so fast… Which was confusing and maddening. "Here I thought Nick wasn't what I wanted. Instead, apparently, I'm not the woman for him."

"Clearly, the man is out of his mind."

"To be fair, he told me several times he didn't want to hurt me." Cinnamon laughed without humor. "And yet, he did. I wish he'd explain himself. He's hiding something, but I can't force him to open up." She stared into the deep red liquid in her glass, as opaque as Nick's secrets.

"Well, fudge." Fran plucked the wine bottle from the coffee table and refilled both glasses. "I suppose this means you're leaning toward taking the job in Boston?"

"I don't want to. I love this town, and I'm tempted to take the general manager's job. Or I was. The possibility of running into Nick anytime, anywhere would be uncomfortable at best. Plus, I truly want to meet someone, get married, and start a family. There aren't a lot of eligible guys around here." Even if there were, the only man she wanted was Nick.

Fran blew out a defeated sigh. "I'm so disappointed.

The mayor and everyone else will truly be sorry to lose you. We all love you."

"Not everyone," Cinnamon corrected. "First thing tomorrow, I'm calling Boston and accepting their offer."

MONDAY AFTERNOON SHARON barged into the workshop behind Nick's bungalow without knocking. "I've been trying to reach you for hours," she said as he slid off the adjustable bar stool he'd converted to a work seat. "Where have you been?"

"Where do you think?" he snarled, gesturing at the machine parts spread on his worktable.

"You're in a crappy mood. You could have answered my calls or at least texted."

In no mood to see or talk with anyone, he'd shut his phone off. "I've been too busy for that."

She gave a terse nod, her eyes upset and her face pale. Now he was worried. "Did something happen to Abby? She was okay when I dropped her at school this morning."

"She's fine."

He heaved a relieved sigh. "What's got you all worked up?" he asked, pushing the stool toward his sister.

Ignoring the invitation to sit down, she crossed her arms and leaned against the wall, between the pegged tool board and a bin of spare parts. "Did you know Cinnamon took the job in Boston?"

He'd kept to himself all day, and hadn't heard. "Did she?"

He sounded as calm as the sea when the tide was out, but he felt as if he'd been punched in the gut. Grabbing a broom from beside the lone window, he began to sweep the concrete floor.

"She's leaving in a couple of days. Who's going to run the factory? We need her." Sharon glared at him. "This is your fault, Nick."

"Mine?" He snorted, the broom kicking up sawdust and debris. "I don't know what you're talking about."

"At the dance Saturday night, you only had eyes for each other. You took her home, and you both looked darned pleased with yourselves. Something must've happened, because you canceled Sunday dinner with Abby and me for no reason.

"Then this morning, Cinnamon accepted a job across the country instead of the one she was offered right here in town. I don't like that, but it's a good job and she ought to be happy. Instead she hung around the factory all day, moping around and snapping at people. I'm no rocket scientist, but I'm not an idiot, either. There's a definite connection between your rotten mood and hers."

While his sister eyed him, he pushed the mess into a neat pile. Cinnamon loved him, or thought she did. That was the connection, but he wasn't going to tell Sharon.

"What did you do to her?"

Made love twice—best sex of his life. He grabbed the dustpan from the its place under the window. "That, big sister, is my business."

"Did you tell her how you feel about her?"

"Again, none of your business." He swept the debris into the dustpan.

"You didn't tell her you love her."

"Nope, because I don't," he said, dumping the pan into the trash bin.

"Oh, yes you do. I'm your sister and I know you, Nick. You're wild about her."

"Bullshit," he muttered, but he sounded uncertain even to his own ears.

He leaned the broom against the wall. "I like her," he conceded, returning the dustpan to its place, "but I'm not right for her."

"Ah." Understanding dawned on his sister's face, and she pushed away from the wall. "I get it. You're afraid to tell her about the dyslexia. It's not a big deal, Nick."

He narrowed his eyes in warning. "Easy to say—you can read."

"So can you. It just takes longer."

He didn't have an answer to that, so he glared at her. "Are you through lecturing me? 'Cause I have work to do."

His sister shook her head. "You're just going to let Cinnamon go, then?"

"Yep." But the thought of never seeing her again made him feel sick.

"Then you're an idiot and a fool."

Chapter Twenty-Five

YOU'RE AN IDIOT and a fool. The words echoed in Nick's brain for the rest of the day and half the night.

After tossing and turning and fighting himself for hours, he realized Sharon was right. He was an idiot and a fool, and tired of hiding his secret. She was right about something else too.

He was in love with Cinnamon.

Crazy, lifetime-together in love. Admitting the truth felt pretty damn good. Make that amazing.

His heart was so full he thought it might burst from his chest if he held his feelings in. He'd drive to Fran's in the morning, tell Cinnamon everything, and ask her to stay.

At the thought, his stomach balled into a hard fist of fear and tension knotted his shoulders. But if this was going to work, and there were no guarantees about that, she had to know the truth.

Unable to rest or work, he prowled restlessly through the house until six. An hour later, showered and shaved, he phoned his sister.

"What do you want, Nick?" she said, sounding testy.

He didn't blame her. "I was a jerk yesterday."

He could almost see her grudging shrug. "You can't help it if you're a bonehead."

"So now I'm boneheaded too?" He chuckled. "Prepare to be shocked. You're right."

"Huh?"

Taking advantage of the confusion that rendered her speechless and stopped her from pestering him with questions, he rushed on. "Can you get someone else to take Abby to school today?"

"That depends on your reasons."

He sucked in a calming breath that didn't do squat. "I'm going over to the Oceanside to talk to Cinnamon."

"At this hour?"

Nick frowned. "What happened to 'Good luck, Nick'?"

His sister chuckled. "Good luck, Nick. Only you don't need it. She loves you, brother. But do me a favor and up the odds by waiting an hour."

Exactly sixty minutes later, nervous as a kid about to read aloud in class, he parked outside the Oceanside. At the front door, he rolled his shoulders to relieve the tension. He couldn't have said whether it worked. He knocked.

After what seemed a good long while, the door opened. Still in her robe, Fran didn't hide her surprise. "Nick." She beckoned him inside. "I didn't expect to see you today, but I can dig up work for you." Her gaze roved from his sports coat to his good pants. "What are you doing in your dress clothes?"

"No work for me today," he said. "I'm here to see Cinnamon." He cleared his throat. "That is, if she's awake."

Fran nodded. "We just finished breakfast. She's upstairs, packing. She doesn't leave till the day after tomorrow, but you know how she is about organizing things."

"She's not going anywhere if I can help it."

His heart in his throat, he headed up the stairs.

ALTHOUGH CINNAMON'S DOOR was open, Nick knocked on the frame and hesitated in the hallway. "It's Nick," he called out. "Can I come in?"

She entered the sitting room from the bedroom, wide-eyed with surprise. "Sure. Why are you all dressed up?"

"We'll get to that in a minute." Shutting the door behind him, he noted the books all over the place.

Books she carried with her to read. Books he'd never crack open.

She picked up a paperback and hugged it to her chest. "What do you want?"

"Better sit down. I have something to say."

After darting a nervous glance around, she chose the oversize armchair.

His legs shook so badly, his knees nearly crumpled. "I think I'll sit too."

He pulled out the desk chair and seated himself behind the desk. Her laptop was there. He closed it and placed it on the floor. Hands folded in her lap—not fidgeting, he noted—Cinnamon eyed him, her expression both wary and hopeful.

Which made things worse. Recalling his advice to Abby about staying calm, he pulled in a fortifying breath, then slowly exhaled. Another breath, and he forged ahead.

"The other night you asked what I was hiding." Though the top button of his shirt was open, his throat felt constricted. He stuck his fingers inside his collar and tugged at it. "This is something about me no one but

Sharon knows about. I'm tired of the secrecy."

Wishing he'd never come over and at the same time wanting to get to the point, he cleared his throat and plunged ahead. "I don't read so well. I have dyslexia."

He braced for her shock, but it didn't come. She looked relieved.

"That's your big, dark secret?" She actually smiled. "I thought maybe you'd been in prison or something."

"Not being able to read is a type of prison. I barely made it through high school." He shifted on the hard, wooden seat. "I didn't graduate until I was twenty years old."

"That must've been painful," she said, not with pity, but with understanding.

"And then some. A lot of kids called me dumb." He looked at her straight-on. "If you're not interested in me anymore, so be it."

She gaped at him as if he'd spoken gibberish. "Silly man, I didn't fall in love with you because I thought you could read. I fell in love with you because you're warm and thoughtful and you have a solid gold heart. And because you're smart."

"You're the smart one. You have a master's degree."

"You don't need an advanced degree to be smart, Nick. I couldn't invent things or fix machines the way you do. That takes brains."

Her belief in him set his soul free. He wasn't stupid, he was smart. The tension stiffening his muscles eased, and he relaxed. "It doesn't bother you that I barely graduated high school?"

She shook her head, her eyes filled with love. "I care about you, not your education."

They stood at the same time.

"You asked why I dressed up," he said. "It's not every day you tell a woman you love her. I love you, Cinnamon."

As she moved toward him, she stumbled over a shoe. He caught her before she fell. "There you go again, tripping. You need me around to keep an eye on you and drive you to Doc's if necessary. Don't take that job in Boston. Stay here with me."

Her eyes filled. Scared out of his wits, he clasped her hands. "That is, if you're okay with living in Dunlin Shores. I guess I could move if—"

"I don't want to move," she said. "I love this town and my new friends. I love Fran. And I love you."

He kissed her. Minutes later, he tore his mouth from hers. "Maybe we should get married."

"Yes—someday."

"You're not ready, and that's okay We can still be

together."

"Let's wait a year. Then, if you still feel this way…"

"I know what I want—to spend the rest of my life with you, and have a few kids together. Through the good and the bad."

"I'm in. I love you, Nick." Her whole face lit up before she went into planning mode. "Where's my phone? I have to call Boston and cancel, then contact the mayor, and—"

"That stuff can wait." He led her to the bedroom, lifted her open suitcase from the unmade bed, and set in the corner. "Right now, I want to make love with the woman I can't live without."

And he did.

THE END

For an update of new releases, sign up for my newsletter here or write me at ann@annroth.net.
bit.ly/2WxhNQT

Get the other books in this series

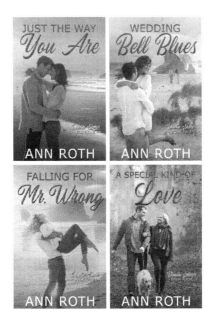

Visit me at Facebook
facebook.com/AnnRothAuthorPage
Follow me on Twitter @Ann_Roth
Email me at ann@annroth.net
Visit my website www.annroth.net

Other books written by Ann Roth

Contemporary Romance

Heroes of Rogue Valley
Mr. January
Mr. February
Mr. March
Mr. April
Mr. May
Mr. June
Mr. July
Mr. August
Mr. September
Mr. December

Halo Island
All I Want for Christmas
The Pilot's Woman
Ooh, Baby!

Ann Roth Classics
A Place to Belong
Father of the Year

Women's Fiction
Another Life
My Sisters

About Ann

Award-winning author Ann Roth writes small town, contemporary romance and women's fiction. She has published over 35 novels, as well as short stories and novellas, both through New York publishers and independently.

A true believer in love and happy endings, Ann enjoys watching her characters learn and grow as they face challenges and hurdles, and ultimately find love.

Ann has lived in the greater Seattle area since she headed for the University of Washington and fell in love with Seattle… and her future husband.

Enjoy!

Made in the USA
Middletown, DE
28 May 2019